Demi Ryder

A Surprise Pregnancy Mafia Romance

This is a work of fiction. Names, characters, organizations, places, events, and incidents are either products of the author's imagination or are used fictitiously.

Copyright © 2024 by Demi Ryder

All rights reserved.

No portion of this book may be reproduced in any form without written permission from the publisher or author, except as permitted by U.S. copyright law.

Contents

Blurb	VII
Prologue	1
Sophia	
1. Chapter One	16
Sophia	
2. Chapter Two	28
Sophia	
3. Chapter Three	35
Angelo	
4. Chapter Four	49
Sophia	
5. Chapter Five	62
Angelo	

6. Chapter Six — Sophia — 74
7. Chapter Seven — Sophia — 84
8. Chapter Eight — Angelo — 91
9. Chapter Nine — Sophia — 101
10. Chapter Ten — Angelo — 108
11. Chapter Eleven — Sophia — 122
12. Chapter Twelve — Sophia — 127
13. Chapter Thirteen — Angelo — 145
14. Chapter Fourteen — Sophia — 157
15. Chapter Fifteen — Angelo — 174
16. Chapter Sixteen — Sophia — 188

17.	Chapter Seventeen Angelo	200
18.	Chapter Eighteen Sophia	213
19.	Chapter Nineteen Angelo	224
20.	Chapter Twenty Sophia	232
21.	Chapter Twenty-One Angelo	244
22.	Chapter Twenty-Two Sophia	252
23.	Chapter Twenty-Three Angelo	261
24.	Chapter Twenty-Four Sophia	267

Epilogue 273
Sophia

Extended Epilogue 279
Sophia

Sneak Peek - Chapter One 288
Surprise Baby for the Mafia Boss

About the Author 299

BLURB

DEMI RYDER

She was promised to me.
A mafia princess who thought she could escape the underworld.
No one gets out of this twisted game...Especially when they're carrying my heir.

There's only one way to keep her safe now—she must play the part...my fiancée.
But I see how she looks at me. She hates me.

Before long I'll have her beneath me, begging for more.
I don't play nice, and I never lose.

I'll groom her into what she was always meant to be—my queen.
She was born to rule beside me in this bloody empire.

Every look of defiance only fuels the fire between us.
But she's hiding something—I'm not blind.
Her belly is growing, sealing our bond in blood.

She's mine—forever. And she knows it.

Prologue

SOPHIA

I was seven years old when my mother taught me how to disappear.

I sat on the edge of my pink, sparkly queen-sized bed, its frills bouncing each time I moved. It was a bed made for fairy tales, but the lesson my mom was teaching me wasn't part of any storybook.

"Always keep your passport in your purse, Sophia. It must stay up to date." Her voice trembled slightly, but her dark eyes were firm.

"And cash, Sophia, always have cash on hand, at least five thousand dollars. Keep a packed suitcase, something light and easy to carry. Have alternate IDs on hand, driver's license, name cards, everything. And finally, *Mia Dolce*, always, always be brave."

I'm sure running away from her husband and the life she had been living for years wasn't something that was on her bucket list, but fate, that unpredictable bitch, had a way of screwing up even the best-laid plans.

The vanishing skill wasn't a skill she'd probably ever intended to pass on, but life has a way of pushing lessons onto us whether we're ready for them or not.

The day had started like any other, with the morning sun spilling through the curtains of our Parisian hotel room, painting everything in a warm, golden light.

I had been excited because we were supposed to go see the Eiffel Tower that day, something I had been looking forward to since we arrived in France. It was a dream for any child—one of those magical landmarks you only ever see in books or on TV.

But there would be no trip to the Eiffel Tower that day.

Instead, after we left the hotel, my mother sat me down on the edge of a chair in a dingy little bread shop, her hands trembling slightly as she brushed a stray curl from my forehead. "Sophia," she began, her voice soft but urgent, "we're going to do something different today."

I remember how I frowned, my young mind struggling to comprehend the shift in her tone. There was something in her eyes that I hadn't seen before, a mixture of fear and resolve that made my chest tighten with a sense of foreboding.

"What about the Eiffel Tower?" I asked, trying to keep the disappointment out of my voice.

She took a deep breath, forcing a smile that didn't quite reach her eyes. "We'll see it another time, sweetheart. Today, we have something important to do. We have to leave France."

"Why aren't we staying in France, Mama?" I asked, my voice small and unsure.

She didn't answer immediately. Instead, she focused on the man seated at a corner table, who looked just as out of place as we did. His suit was sharp, his expression sharper. He wore dark sunglasses and seemed to be looking at us, but I couldn't be sure.

"Because, *Mia Dolce*," she finally said, crouching down to my level as she fished through an envelope, "we're going to play a game."

"A game?" I echoed, intrigued despite the fear gnawing at my insides.

"Yes, a game," she said with a forced smile. "We're going to pretend to be different people for a while. You're going to be Sarah Lacey and I'm going to be Jennifer Lacey. Doesn't that sound fun?"

I didn't think it sounded fun at all. I liked my name, Sophia. I liked being who I was. But I nodded because I could see the plea in her eyes, the silent begging for me to just go along with things.

I nodded again, this time with more certainty. As long as I had her, nothing else mattered. She was my world, my anchor in the storm. I could pretend, for her.

As much as I wanted to be silent and go along with whatever scheme my mama had concocted, I needed answers. Even at seven, I could not stand the thought of being in the dark, on anything.

"What kind of game is this mama? Why are we playing it?"

"It's the kind where we pretend to be different people," she explained, her voice faltering slightly. "Just for a little while, until it's safe."

I remember how my small fingers twisted in my lap, trying to make sense of what she was telling me. "But why do we have to pretend?"

Her smile wavered, and for the first time, I saw tears welling up in her eyes.

It was the first time I'd seen my mother cry and it terrified me. She was always so strong, so unshakable. But in that moment, I could see the cracks in her armor.

"Because sometimes," she said, her voice barely above a whisper, "it's the only way to protect the people we love."

I didn't fully understand what she meant, but I nodded anyway. If pretending meant keeping us safe, then I would do it. For her.

She reached out and gently squeezed my hands, her grip firm despite the tremor in her fingers. "You're so brave, Sophia. So much braver than I ever was."

I shook my head, not wanting to believe that my mother could ever be afraid of anything. "But you're the bravest person I know, Mama."

She let out a shaky laugh, brushing a tear from her cheek with the back of her hand. "We all have to be brave sometimes, my love. Now, let's get ready."

She stood up and rifled quickly through our bags with a speed and efficiency that told me she had done this before—too many times, perhaps.

I watched in silence as she carefully refolded our clothes and tucked them away, reorganizing our already packed bag, her movements quick and practiced. It was as if she was racing against some invisible clock, trying to stay ahead of whatever was chasing us.

As she worked, she spoke in a low, urgent voice, explaining the rules of our game. "From now on, you're not Sophia Agostini anymore," she said, glancing over at me as she locked the suitcase. "You're Sarah Lacey. Can you remember that?"

I nodded, my heart pounding in my chest. "Sarah Lacey," I repeated, the name feeling strange and foreign on my tongue.

"And I'm your mother," she continued, her voice trembling slightly, "Jennifer Lacey. We're just two ordinary people from England, traveling through Europe."

I swallowed hard, the enormity of what she was asking me to do starting to sink in. "But what about Papa?" I asked, my voice barely a whisper.

The mention of my father made her pause, her hands hesitating as she bent to pick up the bag. For a moment, I thought she might cry again, but she quickly blinked back the tears and forced another smile. "We won't be seeing Papa anymore, sweetheart."

"Why not?" I pressed, my confusion growing. I barely knew my father—he was always busy, always away on business. But he was still my father and the thought of never seeing him again filled me with a strange, hollow sadness.

"It's complicated," she said, her voice tight. "But it's for the best."

I didn't understand, but I didn't argue. I could see how much this was hurting her and I didn't want to make it any harder.

Once the bags were organized, she took my hand and led me out onto the street, her grip so tight that it almost hurt. We walked through the bustling streets of Paris, the sound of laughter and conversation filling the air as tourists milled about, oblivious to the fear that was gnawing at my insides.

I kept glancing up at her, searching her face for any sign that this was just another one of our adventures, but all I saw was the tension in her jaw, the way her eyes darted around, as if she was expecting someone to leap out at us from the shadows.

We arrived at a small, unassuming café, where a man in a dark suit was waiting for us.

He looked ordinary enough, but there was something about him that made the hair on the back of my neck stand up. Maybe it was the way his eyes never seemed to settle on one spot for long, or the way he kept glancing at the door as if he was expecting trouble.

My mother greeted him with a tight smile, her voice clipped as she exchanged a few words with him in Italian. I didn't understand most of what they were saying, but I caught a few words here and there—enough to know that this man was helping us escape.

He handed her a small envelope and a package, nodding once before slipping away into the crowd without another word. My mother watched him go, her expression unreadable, before turning her attention back to me.

"Let's go, Sarah," she said, her voice firmer now.

I took her hand, letting her lead me out of the café and back onto the busy street. The sun was shining, but it felt cold—colder than it should have been. I shivered, clutching my mother's hand as if it were the only thing keeping me anchored to the ground.

As we walked, she began talking to me about our new life in England, painting a picture of a world that seemed far removed from the one we were leaving behind.

"You're going to love London," she said, her voice lighter now, as if she was trying to convince herself as much as she was convincing me. "There are so many things to see—the Tower of London, Big Ben, the red double-decker buses…"

"And the queen!" I added, trying to match her enthusiasm, though my heart wasn't in it.

"Yes, the queen," she agreed, her smile a little more genuine this time. "We're going to have so much fun, Sarah."

But even as she spoke, I could see the worry etched into her features, the way her eyes kept flicking back over her shoulder as if she expected someone to be following us.

I tried to imagine what our new life would be like, but it was difficult. England was just a place on a map to me, a distant land that I'd only ever heard about in stories. But now, it was going to be my home. A place where I would have to forget about Sophia Agostini and become Sarah Lacey, a girl with a different name and a different life.

I clung to her hand as we made our way to the train station, my mind racing with questions I didn't know how to ask. What were we running from? Why couldn't we stay in France? Why couldn't we go back to New York, to the life we'd always known?

But I didn't ask any of those questions. I was too afraid of what the answers might be.

At the train station, she guided me to a quiet corner where we sat on a bench, waiting for our train. The envelope and package the man had given her lay on her lap and I watched as she slowly opened the envelope, revealing a set of passports and documents.

"Look," she said, holding up one of the passports for me to see. "This is you now, Sarah."

I took the passport from her, staring at the picture inside. It was me, but it wasn't me. The name beside the photo read "Sarah Lacey" and for a moment, I felt like I was looking at a stranger.

"This is who you are now," she said, her voice gentle but firm. "You need to remember that, no matter what happens."

I nodded, clutching the passport tightly in my hands. "I will, Mama. I'll remember."

She smiled, but there was a sadness in her eyes that made my chest ache. "You're such a good girl, Sophia. I'm so proud of you."

"Sarah," I corrected her, trying to embrace my new identity. "I'm Sarah now."

Her smile widened and she brushed a kiss against my forehead. "Yes, Sarah. My brave, beautiful Sarah."

We sat there in silence for a while, the noise of the bustling train station fading into the background as I tried to process everything that had happened.

My world had shifted on its axis and nothing felt real anymore. I was no longer Sophia Agostini, the daughter of a powerful man in New York. I was Sarah Lacey, a girl on the run with her mother, hiding from a past I didn't fully understand.

The train arrived with a loud, screeching halt and my mother stood up, taking my hand as we walked towards it. I glanced back over my shoulder one last time, at the life we were leaving behind, and felt a pang of loss in my chest.

I didn't know if I would ever see France again, or if I would ever understand why we had to leave.

But I knew one thing for certain—I had to be strong, for my mother's sake. She was all I had now, and I couldn't let her down.

We boarded the next train and found our seats quickly. As the train pulled away from the station, I pressed my face against the window, watching the city blur into the distance. My mother sat beside me, her hand resting on mine, her grip firm and steady.

"Remember, Sarah," she whispered, her voice barely audible over the rumble of the train. "This is just a game. We're going to win it, you and me."

I turned to look at her, searching her eyes for reassurance. "What happens when the game is over?"

She didn't answer right away. Instead, she reached out and tucked a strand of hair behind my ear, her expression softening. "When it's over, we'll be safe. We'll have a new life, a better life."

I nodded, trying to believe her. But deep down, I knew that nothing would ever be the same again.

As the train carried us further away from Paris, from everything I had ever known, I closed my eyes and tried to imagine our new life in England. I pictured the red buses, the tall buildings, the parks and the people with accents that were different from ours. I imagined myself as Sarah Lacey, a girl with no past, only a future.

***

The apartment was quiet that night, save for the occasional hum of the city filtering through the window. I had just drifted into sleep when a loud, piercing scream jolted me awake.

My heart pounded in my chest as I scrambled out of bed, my small hands clutching my stuffed rabbit as I stumbled toward my mother's room.

The door was ajar, and I peered inside to see her thrashing about in bed, her face contorted with terror. "He's coming! He's coming!" she cried, her voice high and frantic. The words made no sense to me, but the fear in her tone was palpable.

"Mama!" I called, stepping into the room. I tried to shake her awake, my tiny hands barely making an impact. "Mama, wake up!"

Her eyes flew open, and she looked at me with a mix of confusion and fear. She sat up abruptly, her breathing ragged. "Sophia? Sarah?" she stammered, her gaze darting around as if she was searching for something unseen.

"It's all right, Mama," I said, my voice trembling. I climbed onto the bed and hugged her tightly. "It was just a dream. It was just a bad dream."

She took a deep breath, slowly coming back to the present. Her shaking hands brushed away the tears that had streaked her face. "I'm sorry, darling," she whispered, her voice hoarse. "I didn't mean to scare you."

"It's okay," I reassured her, though I wasn't sure if I believed it myself. "You're safe now."

She nodded and held me close, her trembling subsiding as she calmed down. "Thank you, Sarah," she said softly. "I'm sorry I woke you."

Over the next few weeks, the nightmares became a recurring presence in our lives.

Each night, my mother would wake in terror and I would be there beside her, offering comfort and a semblance of safety. I never quite understood what haunted her, but I could see the toll it took on her. Her once-bright eyes were often shadowed with worry and the corners of her mouth were set in a permanent frown.

Despite the fear, life had to go on. My mother started working at a small but busy café in the heart of London. It wasn't much, but it was enough to keep us afloat. The café was a quaint place with red and white checkered tablecloths and a chalkboard menu that advertised "tea and scones" and "full English breakfast" for a few pounds.

I began attending school at a local primary school. The accents and customs were different from what I was used to and it took me a while to adjust. One day, a group of children began teasing me about my American accent, calling me names and making fun of the way I spoke.

"Look at her! She's a proper yank," one of the kids sneered, his tone dripping with derision. *Yank*. It amused me more than insulted me, probably because I didn't know what it meant.

"Is she deaf too?"

Just then, a girl with a pixie cut and a mischievous sparkle in her eyes, stepped in front of me, glaring at the bullies. "Oi, leave her alone," she said firmly, her London accent thick and unapologetic. "She's new here. Give her a break. You fancy another broken nose, Tommy?"

The one who had shoved me, the one I assumed was Tommy, turned a concerning shade of purple and they bolted. Well, well.

I watched, wide-eyed, as the girl, Justine I think her name was, stood up to the bullies with a confidence I could only dream of. After they scurried off, she turned to me with a warm smile. "You all right?" she asked.

I nodded, feeling a rush of gratitude. "Don't worry, they're just a bunch of wankers. My daddy says I shouldn't say that because it's a bad word, but Uncle Sam calls everyone wankers. I reckon it's maybe not so bad a word, do you think?"

"I don't know what it means," I said softly. "I'm Sarah."

"Nice to meet you, Sarah," she said with a grin. "I'm Justine. Don't worry 'bout those muppets. They'll get bored of picking on you soon."

Justine and I became fast friends. She introduced me to her favorite hangouts—a tiny ice cream parlor that let you create new ice cream flavors and name them yourself, and an amusement park where most of the rides were broken.

We'd sit and talk about everything from school to our favorite cartoons. Through her friendship, I began to feel more at home in London.

And so, as London continued to reveal its wonders and challenges, my mother and I faced the hard times together, determined to carve out a place for ourselves in a city that was beginning to feel like home.

But no matter how hard I tried, I couldn't shake the feeling that the game we were playing was more dangerous than my mother was letting on. And I couldn't help but wonder—what would happen if we lost?

Chapter One

Sophia

Death is a cruel thief, stealing the vibrancy from life and leaving behind only echoes of what once was. It settles over us like a heavy cloak, muffling the sounds of joy and laughter until only faint whispers of memories remain.

The end is a constant shadow that stretches longer and darker with each passing day, a stark reminder of our fleeting existence.

As I stand by my mother's bedside, the dim hospital room feels colder, the silence heavier. The steady beep of the heart monitor is a harsh reminder of the finality that lies just ahead. Each beep grows fainter, as if the machine itself is reluctant to let go. I watch as my mother's once-vibrant face pales, the life slowly slipping away from her frail body.

I want to reach out, to hold her hand and reassure her that everything will be okay, but I'm paralyzed by the enormity of this moment.

Her eyes flutter open, and she looks at me with a clarity I haven't seen in weeks. "Sophia," she whispers, her voice barely audible. The name hits me like a jolt. "Mom, it's Sarah," I correct her softly, my heart aching. I've spent years building a new identity, a shield against the world I left behind. In this moment, her calling me Sophia is a painful reminder of what I've tried so hard to forget.

Her gaze turns wistful, her tears mixing with the pain etched on her face. "I failed you," she says, her voice cracking. "I should have never lied to you. I should have told you everything."

I'm stunned, my breath catching in my throat. "Mom, I don't understand. What are you talking about?" I ask, desperate for answers that seem just beyond her reach.

"There's something you don't know," she begins, her voice trailing off. The effort of speaking seems to drain her, and she struggles to keep her eyes open. "Something I've been keeping from you. We made a promise, we promised he could have you. I didn't want to, but your father made me agree. He will come for you. He will come..."

Her voice fades until it's barely a whisper. Her eyes close, and the room is enveloped in a suffocating silence. The beeping of the monitor stops, and I'm left with the crushing weight of her final, unspoken words.

What did she mean? Was she just lost in her own thoughts and talking about my father? She had seemed so lucid, however, so clear.

I felt a chill pass over me and I shuddered as I looked at her lifeless body. Nurses came into the room, softly touching my shoulder and guiding me to step back so they could check on the machines and verify that my mother was gone.

I barely registered their presence, my mind spinning. Who was coming for me? And why?

***

The sky wept as we laid my mother to rest. It was the kind of steady, relentless rain that soaked you to the bone, a miserable backdrop to an already miserable day. I stand at the graveside, clutching a small bouquet of white lilies, the scent sharp and sweet in the damp air.

My black dress clings to my skin, heavy with rain, but I barely notice. I am numb, detached from everything except the hollow ache in my chest.

The priest's voice drones on, a low murmur of prayers and scripture that I can't bring myself to focus on. My gaze is fixed on the coffin as it is slowly lowered into the ground, a box too small to hold all the memories, the love, the life that had been my mother. A sob threatens to escape, but I swallow it down, refusing to break. Not here. Not now.

Justine stands beside me, her arm looped through mine, offering silent support. I feel the gentle pressure of her grip, grounding me as everything else spins out of control. She is the only one here who really knows what I am going through—the only one who knows the truth about who I am and the life I have left behind.

"It's okay to cry, Sarah," she whispers, using the name I had lived under for so many years.

To her, I would always be Sarah, the friend she had met in school, the one who shared late-night study sessions and whispered secrets. Justine didn't know Sophia, not really, but she knew enough to understand the weight of the moment.

"I know," I reply, my voice barely audible over the rain. "I just...I don't want to."

"You don't have to be strong all the time," she says, squeezing my arm gently. "Not today."

But I did. I had to be strong because my mother was gone, and without her, I felt like a ship lost at sea, adrift and vulnerable. I couldn't afford to fall apart now. Not with everything I had to face.

"We are here today to say goodbye to Jennifer Lacey," the priest intones. "A mother, a friend, a cherished soul who touched many lives. May her memory be a blessing, and may we find solace in the knowledge that she is at peace."

The floral arrangements surrounding the grave are a sea of white lilies and roses, their delicate petals glistening with raindrops. The headstones nearby stand like silent sentinels, each telling a story of a life once lived. The ground is soft and wet, the air filled with the earthy scent of fresh soil and flowers.

The drizzling rain patters softly against the black umbrella that barely shields me from the chill. As I stand beside the freshly dug grave, the weight of my mother's death presses down on me like the leaden sky above. The finality of it all—this is the last time I'll see her, the last time I'll hear her voice, the last whisper of the secrets she carried with her.

My fingers grip the handful of dirt, and I let it fall onto the casket, mixing with the countless others that have already piled up. The dirt lands with a muted thud, and I fight to keep my composure, biting my lip until the sting brings tears to my eyes.

As the final words of the eulogy fade into the rain, I step forward, my heels sinking into the wet earth. The lilies tremble in my hands as I stare down at the grave, the reality of it all crashing over me like a tidal wave. She was really gone. The one person who had always been there, my anchor in the storm, was gone.

I drop the flowers into the grave, watching as they land softly on the casket. My vision blurs, tears mingling with the rain, and for a moment, I thought I might collapse under the weight of it all. Justine's grip tightened on my arm, steadying me, and I leaned into her support, grateful for her presence.

"I'm here," she murmured, her voice a soft comfort in the storm. "You're not alone, Sarah."

But I felt alone. Even with Justine beside me, I felt a void that no one could fill. The secrets of my past, the life I had hidden from everyone—including her—were now mine to bear alone.

As I step back from the grave, a figure catches my eye through the veil of rain. A man, tall and imposing, stands at a distance, watching the proceedings with an intensity that makes my breath catch in my throat. He's dressed in a dark, tailored suit, his black hair slicked back, the rain beading on the surface without disturbing its perfect style. I note that he wears glasses, and my scrambled brain suddenly thinks of Clark Kent and superheroes hiding in plain sight.

Everything about him screams power and control, and as his gaze meets mine, I feel a jolt of recognition.

"Do you know him?" Justine asks, following my gaze.

I shake my head slowly, but my heart knows better. There is something familiar about him, something that tugs at the edges of my memory. I can't place him, but I know in my bones that I should be afraid.

The man starts walking toward us, his movements deliberate and unhurried. My pulse quickens as he closes the distance, his green eyes locked onto mine with an intensity that leaves no room for escape or breath.

He turns to me, his eyes meeting mine with a calm that feels oddly unsettling. "My name is Angelo," he says, offering his hand. "I've been looking forward to meeting you, Sophia."

Hearing my name—Sophia— makes me flinch, as if he has just thrown the world's worst profanity at me. I stagger back, and would have toppled right into the grave with my mother if his hands had not shot out and grabbed my waist.

Sparks light up where his fingers connect with my exposed skin, and I shiver involuntarily. His gaze is merciless on me, unrelenting, as if he is daring me to look away first. *Sorry Angelo. If there's one thing I'm good at, it's playing games and coming out victorious.*

"How do you know my name?" I ask, trying to keep my voice steady.

"I know quite a bit about you." His tone carries an unsettling mix of certainty and something else that sends a shiver down my spine.

I glance at Justine, who is still chatting quietly with a few remaining guests. "Justine, could you please get me some tea from inside?" I ask, hoping to buy myself some time. "I'll join you shortly."

Justine looks at me with a hint of concern but nods. "Sure, love. I'll be right back." She heads toward the house, leaving Angelo and I alone by the grave.

The silence between us feels charged and heavy. My heart is beating too fast. I think that maybe it's trying to make up for my mother's which is still forever now.

"Who are you?"

"You are many things Sophia, but stupid is not one of them. You know who I am." He's right. Of course, I know who he is. Well, at least I know of him. He's the boogeyman of the underworld.

"Don't call me that. My name is Sarah."

"Is that what she had you believe?" He takes a step, and just like that, he's too close to me. His scent invades my nostrils, swimming in the air around me until all I can smell is him. All I can see is him. I feel a sudden urge to collapse into his arms and I cringe away from the idea right off. What is wrong with me?

"You're good at pretending, but nobody is that good, Sophia."

I was not about to fall for his trap, not after everything my mother did to keep us safe.

"If you aren't going to tell me who you are, leave. This is a gathering of family and friends only. You're neither of those things."

His eyes lock with mine again, and he nudges his glasses back into place with an elegant finger. I was sure that he would call my bluff, but then he just nods.

He reaches into his coat and hands me a small card, his expression unreadable. "Fine. I'll play. Angelo Castiglia. I'm sorry for your loss."

My heart skips a beat at the name—Castiglia. It's a name that was whispered in the shadows during my childhood. It's a name that carries weight and fear. My stomach twists into knots as I stare at the card, the letters blurring in front of my eyes.

"Doesn't ring a bell," I lie. "Were you a friend of my mother's?"

"I was a friend of your father's."

That sent a chill down my spine, and he must've seen the fear in my eyes because he moves in closer, like a predator stalking his prey.

"Why are you here?" I ask softly, trying to steady my voice. "What do you want from me?" It was useless to push my luck with the games now.

"I need to talk to you," he insists. "Not here. Later."

"There's nothing for us to talk about." I try to walk away but he grabs my arm. Not hard enough to hurt, but enough to let me know that he could cause unimaginable pain should he so desire.

"I'm not your enemy. I'm not here to fight. Twenty minutes is all I need."

I hesitate, my heart pounding in my chest. Every instinct screams at me to run, to get as far away from this man as possible. But there is something about the way he looks at me, something that makes it clear he isn't asking.

"Please," he adds, his voice softening. "It's important."

With trembling fingers, I take the card from his hand. It's plain, with nothing but his name and a location scrawled in elegant script on it. I glance up at him, my mind a whirlwind of confusion and fear.

"Why?" is all I can manage.

"Because you're not safe," he replies, his eyes darkening with an emotion I can't quite name. "There are things you don't know, things you need to understand. Meet me there tonight, and I'll explain everything. After I'm done, if you still want nothing to do with me, I'll leave you alone."

Call it desperate hope, but I'm willing to cling to any silver lining I can at this point. He might not be sincere, but I don't see that I have a choice in any of this. I have to know why he thinks I'm in danger because my mother told me that I was before she died.

He doesn't give me a chance to respond, turning on his heel and walking away with the same quiet confidence that had drawn my attention in the first place.

"What was that about?" Justine asks, her brow furrowed with concern as she returns with two cups of tea in hand.

I shake my head, slipping the card into my pocket. "I'm not sure...but I think I need to find out."

The rain continues to fall, a steady patter against the ground, but I am too lost in my thoughts to care. I look down at the card again, the name Angelo Castiglia burning into my mind. This is bad—really bad. I have spent my entire life running from the world my mother fled, the world of crime and power that had consumed my father. And now, it seemed, that world had found me again.

Justine looks at me, worry etched into her features. "Are you okay?"

I force a smile, though it feels hollow. "I will be."

The funeral ends and I stay behind, waiting until the last of the mourners leave before making my way back to the grave. Justine hovers nearby, giving me space but refusing to leave me alone.

The earth is freshly turned, the hole in the ground an ugly scar on the landscape. I kneel beside it, the dampness seeping through my dress, and let the tears fall freely now that I am alone.

"I'm so sorry, Mama," I whisper, my voice breaking. "I don't know what to do."

The only answer is the rain, relentless and unyielding, just like the world I had tried so hard to escape. But there is no escaping it now. I can feel it in my bones, in the way Angelo looked at me, the way his presence filled the air with unspoken promises.

Justine comes over and kneels beside me, her arm wrapping around my shoulders. "We'll figure it out," she says softly. "Whatever this is, we'll handle it together."

I lean into her, grateful for the comfort of her presence. "Thank you, Justine. I don't know what I'd do without you."

"You don't have to worry about that," she replies with a small smile. "I'm not going anywhere."

We stay like that for a while, just the two of us, the rain our only company. I know that I can't hide from the truth forever, but for a few more moments, I allow myself to believe that everything will be okay. That I'm alone.

But deep down, I know that Angelo's words have shattered that illusion. This is just the beginning of something far bigger, far more dangerous than anything I could ever have imagined.

Chapter Two

SOPHIA

We stay by the grave until the rain lightens to a drizzle.

The cemetery grew quieter, and the mourners dispersed. The stillness around us felt heavy, pressing down on me as I stood, my legs stiff from kneeling on the wet ground.

Justine rose with me, her hand on my back, guiding me away from the grave. "Let's get you home," she says softly, her voice a balm to my frayed nerves. "You need to rest."

Rest. The word felt foreign, impossible even. My mind is too full, spinning with thoughts of my mother's death, of Angelo Castiglia, and of the dangerous past I had thought was buried forever. I want to protest, to tell Justine that rest isn't something I can afford right now, but I'm too exhausted to argue.

She leads me to her car, a small, reliable hatchback that has seen us through countless late-night drives and spontaneous road trips. Today, it's a sanctuary, a small bubble of warmth and familiarity from the cold, uncertain world outside.

Justine drives in silence, the hum of the engine the only sound between us.

I stare out the window, watching the rain blur the cityscape into a wash of gray and black. London has always felt like a safe haven, a place where I can blend in, disappear. But now, with the weight of Angelo's words hanging over me, it feels as foreign and dangerous as the life I left behind.

"Do you want to talk about it?" Justine asks, her eyes flicking toward me before returning to the road.

I hesitate, unsure of how much I could tell her. Justine doesn't know anything about my past. My mother forbade me from saying a word. She always said that I couldn't trust anyone, not while he was still around.

"I'm not sure what there is to say," I reply finally, my voice strained. "It's just…overwhelming."

Justine nods, her lips pressing into a thin line. "That man—Angelo Castiglia—do you know him?"

"Not personally," I say, choosing my words carefully. "But I know of him."

"And you're going to meet him?"

I sigh, rubbing my temples as the headache that has been brewing all day finally begins to surface. "I don't think I have a choice."

Justine glances at me again, her eyes filled with concern. "Sarah, what does he want with you?"

"I don't know," I admit, and that's the truth. I can guess, of course—Angelo Castiglia wouldn't have sought me out if it wasn't something serious, something dangerous. But what exactly he wanted from me, I couldn't say.

"I just want you to be careful," Justine says, her voice filled with worry. "I don't trust him."

I can't help but smile at that, a small, wry smile that holds no humor. "Neither do I."

The rest of the drive passes in silence, each of us lost in our own thoughts. By the time we reach my flat, the rain has stopped entirely, leaving the world damp and glistening in the fading light. Justine parks in front of the building and turns to me, her expression serious.

"Do you want me to stay?" she asks.

For a moment, I'm tempted to say yes. To ask her to stay the night, to fill my small flat with her warmth and chatter, to drown out the noise in my head with the comfort of her presence. But I know that isn't fair. I can't drag her into this any deeper than she already is. This is my mess, my past, and it's up to me to deal with it.

"No, it's okay," I say, forcing a smile. "I'll be fine."

She doesn't look convinced, but she nods anyway. "Call me if you need anything, okay? Anything at all."

"I will. Thank you, Justine. For everything."

She gives me a quick hug, and I cling to her for just a moment, drawing strength from her before pulling away. I watch as she drives off, her car disappearing around the corner, leaving me alone with my thoughts.

I stand there for a few moments, staring up at the building that has been my home for the past few years. It looks the same as it always does—brick facade, tall windows, the familiar, comforting scent of rain-soaked concrete. But now, it feels different. The safety I have always felt here is gone, replaced by a gnawing sense of unease.

The silence is oppressive, wrapping around me like a shroud as I lean against the door, my thoughts racing.

I can't shake the image of Angelo Castiglia from my mind—the way he had looked at me, the quiet power that radiated from him. He was dangerous, I knew that much. But he was also my only link to the world I had left behind, the world my mother had fled to protect me.

I walk through the flat on autopilot, shedding my wet clothes as I go. I toss them into the laundry hamper and pull on a pair of soft, comfortable sweats, wrapping myself in a thick robe. But no amount of comfort can ease the tension coiled tight in my chest.

The card Angelo gave me is still in my pocket, and I pull it out, staring at it as I sink onto the couch. The address is in the city, a nondescript location that could have been anything from a high-end restaurant to an underground club. I have no idea what I will find there, or what Angelo wants with me.

Part of me wants to ignore it, to tear the card in half and throw it away, to pretend that none of this has happened. But I know that isn't an option. Angelo found me, and if he has gone to the trouble of seeking me out, he won't just let me disappear again. Not without answers.

The memory of his voice echoes in my mind—"You're not safe."

Safe. I had lived my life by that word, letting it dictate every choice, every move. But now, it seemed, safety was a luxury I could no longer afford.

With a sigh, I reach for my phone, my fingers trembling as I dial the number on the card. It rings only once before a voice answers, deep and smooth, sending a shiver down my spine.

"Angelo Castiglia."

"It's Sophia," I say, my voice steadier than I felt. "Sophia Agostini."

There's a brief pause, and I can almost hear the shift in his demeanor, the awareness that this is no ordinary call. "Sophia," he repeats, as if testing the name on his tongue. "I wasn't sure you'd call."

"Neither was I," I admit. "But here we are."

"Here we are," he echoes, and I can hear the faintest hint of satisfaction in his tone. "I'm glad you did. There's a lot we need to discuss."

"When?" I ask, my heart pounding in my chest.

"Tonight," he says without hesitation. "Nine o'clock. I'll send a car to pick you up."

"Okay," I agree, knowing that I don't really have a choice. "I'll be ready." I don't bother to ask how he knows where I live. Men like him always know.

"Good," he says, his voice softening just a fraction. "You're doing the right thing, Sophia. I'll see you soon."

The line goes dead, leaving me with nothing but the sound of my own heartbeat echoing in my ears. I drop the phone onto the couch beside me, staring at it as if it might offer some answers to the questions swirling in my mind.

But there are no answers. Only the knowledge that my life is about to change, irrevocably and dangerously. I have spent so many years running, hiding from the ghosts of my past, only to have them catch up to me when I least expected it.

And now, as the clock ticks closer to nine, all I can do is wait. Wait for Angelo Castiglia to take me back into the world I tried so hard to escape. Wait for whatever fate has in store for me.

I take a deep breath, closing my eyes as I lean back against the couch. For the first time since my mother's death, I allow myself to think about the life I left behind. The life of Sophia Agostini, the girl who had been hidden away for so long, only to be thrust back into the light.

The girl who will soon have to face the truth about her family, her past, and herself.

As the minutes tick by, I feel the fear coiling tighter in my chest, but I push it down, focusing on the one thing I know for certain.

I'm going to meet Angelo Castiglia tonight.

And nothing will ever be the same again.

Chapter Three

Angelo

I've always been a man who's been able to take pride in his integrity. My word is my word—always has been and always will be. But today, I lied.

I lied when I told her that if she didn't want anything to do with me, I would let her go. I knew from the second I saw her that I was never going to let her go, not when everything in me screamed her name, calling her mine.

The rain in London was different from the rain in New York. It wasn't the heavy, pounding storm that lashed against windows and turned streets into rivers. It was a quieter, more insidious rain—constant, unrelenting, the kind that seeped into your bones and refused to let go.

I watched it through the window of the small pub where I arranged to meet Sophia. The place was old, the kind of establishment that had seen generations pass through its doors, each one leaving its mark in worn wooden floors and faded wallpaper. It's the perfect spot for a discreet meeting, far from the prying eyes of the city.

I haven't seen her in years, not since she was a child. But I remember her—remember the fierce intelligence in her eyes, the quiet strength that belied her age.

She was her father's daughter, no doubt about that. Carlo Agostini had been a formidable man, one of the few men who had earned my respect in a world where trust was a rare commodity. And now, with Carlo gone, Sophia is the only link left to the Agostini empire.

I take a sip of my whiskey, letting the warmth spread through me as I glance at my watch. She would be here soon, I had no doubt about that. Sophia might have spent years hiding from the life she was born into, but she wasn't a coward. She knew it was time to face the inevitable.

The place was empty, only a single bartender and the telly droning on in the background. A game of soccer—football—was on. I didn't want an audience for the conversation I was about to have with Sophia, so I had all the patrons dismissed for the evening. The owner didn't seem to mind though, not when I paid him twenty thousand pounds for the time.

The door to the pub creaked open, and I look up just in time to see her step inside. The years have been kind to her—too kind, perhaps.

She is beautiful, in a way that is both understated and undeniable. Her dark brown hair is damp from the rain, curling slightly at the ends, and her hazel-green eyes sweep across the room with a mix of wariness and determination. She is dressed simply, in dark jeans and a sweater, but there is an elegance to her that is impossible to ignore.

She spots me almost immediately, and I see the flicker of recognition in her eyes as she makes her way over to my table. Her steps are measured, controlled, as if she is holding herself back from running—whether toward me or away from me, I can't be sure.

"Sophia," I greet her as she approaches, standing to pull out a chair for her. "Thank you for coming."

She hesitates for a moment before sitting down, her posture stiff, her hands clasped tightly in her lap. "I didn't have much of a choice, did I?" she replies, her voice steady, but I can hear the undercurrent of tension in it.

I sit back down across from her, studying her for a moment before responding. "No, you didn't. But I'm glad you made the right decision."

She bristles at that, her eyes narrowing slightly. "And what exactly is the 'right decision', Angelo? Coming here to meet you? Or something else you haven't bothered to tell me yet?"

A faint smile tugs at the corner of my mouth. She's sharp, just like her father. "You're here because there are things you need to know, Sophia. Things that could mean the difference between life and death."

"Like what?" she asks, leaning forward slightly, her gaze intense. "What is it that I need to know so badly?"

"Drink?" I ask, and she shakes her head.

"You probably spiked it with God knows what."

"Don't insult me. If I wanted you in my bed, you'd be in my bed willingly."

She looks at me and swallows again. "It's terribly empty in here. Did your overwhelming darkness send everyone running?"

"I rented the whole place. Didn't think you'd want to have this conversation in public."

"How considerate. Why am I here, Angelo?" I want to close my eyes and savor the sound of my name on her tongue. It's delicious. But not yet, not now.

I take another sip of my drink, letting the silence stretch out between us for a moment. "Your father is dead."

She flinches, the words hitting her like a physical blow. She hadn't known, then. I had suspected as much, but seeing the shock on her face confirmed it.

"When?" Her voice is smaller this time, and I can see the struggle between guilt and grief on her face.

"A week ago."

Her laugh is sardonic.

"There has to be something poetic about both my parents dying at the same time. Was he killed?"

"No. His health had been failing for a long time. Your mother was aware."

"If you're trying to make me feel bad for him…"

"I don't believe in useless emotions like guilt, and I can't abide people who waste their time on it, or mine."

She sighs and leans back in her seat. "I guess I'll be needing that drink after all."

I call for the bartender, and she orders a scotch, which makes me smile.

"I didn't know him," she says after taking a long sip.

"I know. But I did."

"Is this the part where you tell me what a good man he was? Spare me the lecture."

"He wasn't a good man, at least not in the orthodox definition of the word. But he was a fair man."

"That does not make a single difference to me."

"I know," I continue, my voice measured. "That's not why I needed to meet with you, though. His death has left a power vacuum, one that others are all too eager to fill."

She swallows hard, her throat working as she tries to process what I'm telling her. "And what does that have to do with me?" she asks, though I could tell she already knows the answer.

"It has everything to do with you," I say quietly. "You're the only heir to the Agostini family business. With your father gone, you're the one who holds the keys to the entire empire."

She shakes her head, her hands tightening around each other in her lap. "If it wasn't already obvious, I took those keys and chucked them right into the ocean when I ran off with my mother. I haven't been his child for twenty years."

"Time is of no relevance here, Sophia. If I cut your skin, you will bleed Agostini blood. That's all that matters. Whether you like it or not, you're a part of this world, Sophia. And now, with your father gone, you're in more danger than you realize."

Her eyes flick up to meet mine, a mix of fear and defiance burning in their hazel depths. "And you're here to protect me, is that it?"

"I'm here to make sure you stay alive," I correct her. "There are people who would kill to take control of the Agostini family. And if they find you, they will kill you to get it."

The color drains from her face, and for a moment, she looks like she might be sick. But then she squares her shoulders, drawing on that inner strength I had always known she possessed. "So, what's your plan, Angelo? What do you want from me?"

"I want you to come back to New York," I say simply. "It's the only place where I can keep you safe."

She stares at me, disbelief written across her features. "You want me to just...what? Pretend like the last twenty years never happened? Go back to a life I barely even remember?"

"I want you to survive," I say, leaning forward slightly, my voice dropping to a low, insistent tone. "I want you to live, Sophia. And the only way to do that is to come back with me, to take your place in the Agostini family, at least until we can figure out who's trying to take control of your family's business."

She shakes her head again, but there is less conviction in it this time. I can see the wheels turning in her mind, the struggle between her desire for a normal life and the reality of the situation she is in.

"And if I say no?" she asks, her voice quiet.

"Then you'll die," I say bluntly. "It's only a matter of time before they find you. And when they do, they won't give you a choice."

Her breath hitches, and I see the fear flash in her eyes before she looks away, staring down at the table. She is silent for a long moment, and I can almost see the battle playing out in her mind—the longing to stay hidden, to keep the life she had built for herself, warring with the knowledge that it was no longer safe. But I knew her, I knew that a threat to her life would not be enough to change her mind.

"The people who want what you have are ruthless. They will stop at nothing to break you utterly. That includes getting rid of everyone you care about. Everyone."

Her eyes go wide, and she gulps down the remnant of her drink.

Finally, she looks up at me, her expression resigned. "If I do this...if I go back with you...what happens next?"

"I keep you safe," I say, relaxing slightly now that I know I have her. "We figure out who's behind this, and we take them down. And when it's over, if you still want to leave, I'll make sure you can." There's that lie again. It tastes bitter on my tongue, but I swallow down the distaste. I'm trying to protect her. I will stop at nothing to keep her safe.

She studies me for a long moment, searching my face for any sign of deception. I want her safe, yes, but I also want something more—something I'm not quite ready to admit to myself, let alone to her.

"Okay," she says finally, her voice barely above a whisper. "I need some time to think about it."

"Not too long. Time is the one thing I can't afford to give you now."

I signal the bartender for the check, then turn back to her. "I have a car waiting outside. We can leave as soon as you're ready."

She nods, her gaze distant as she processes everything that has just happened. I can see the weight of it settling on her shoulders, the knowledge that her life is about to change in ways she can't yet comprehend.

But she is strong—stronger than she knows. And as much as she will probably hate it, she will rise to the occasion. Of that, I am certain.

We stand up and I gesture for her to follow me. She does, her steps hesitant at first, but growing more confident as we make our way to the door. The rain has picked up again, a steady downpour that soaks through my coat as we step outside.

The car is waiting at the curb, the driver already holding the door open for us. I motion for her to get in, and after a brief pause, she does, sliding into the back seat with a resigned sigh.

I follow her in, closing the door behind me. As the car pulls away from the pub, I glance over at her, noting the way she stares out the window, her expression unreadable.

"Thank you," she says suddenly, her voice barely audible over the sound of the rain.

"For what?" I ask, surprised by the unexpected gratitude.

"For giving me a choice," she replies, still not looking at me. "Even if it wasn't much of one."

I don't respond, unsure of what to say. The truth is, I wasn't sure I had given her a choice at all. I had presented her with the only option that would keep her alive, but I knew it wasn't a path she wanted to take. And yet, she had chosen it anyway, because that was who she was—strong, pragmatic and determined to survive.

As we drive through the rain-soaked streets of London, heading toward the unknown, I can't shake the feeling that this is the beginning of something much bigger than either of us might have imagined.

And for the first time in a long time, I feel a spark of something more than just duty—something I'm not ready to name, but that I still know will change everything.

***

I watch as Sophia disappears into the entrance of her building, her steps hesitant yet determined. She doesn't look back, and I didn't expect her to. She is probably already thinking of ways to avoid seeing me again. But she won't be able to. Not now.

As the door clicks shut behind her, I let out a breath I hadn't realized I was holding. She is safe, for now. But the real challenge is just beginning.

"Take me back to the hotel," I instruct the driver. My voice is steady, betraying none of the turmoil swirling in my chest.

The car pulls away from the curb, gliding through the rain-slicked streets of London. I lean back in my seat, my thoughts still with Sophia, replay every moment of our interaction. She is exactly as I remembered—sharp, stubborn, and more beautiful than any woman had a right to be. But there is something else now, something deeper—a vulnerability she tries so hard to hide. But it's there, simmering just beneath the surface.

It makes me want to protect her, to shield her from the world and all the dangers that are closing in on her. But it also makes me want to break down the walls she's built around herself, to see the woman underneath—the one who is hiding, even from herself.

When we arrive at the hotel, I step out into the drizzle, the cold air a welcome contrast to the heat still lingering inside me from my time with Sophia. The doorman greets me with a respectful nod, holding the door open as I walk inside. The warmth of the lobby envelopes me, but it does nothing to soothe the restlessness gnawing at my insides.

The elevator ride to the top floor is quiet, the kind of silence that magnifies every thought, every doubt. By the time I reach my suite, I'm itching for something to take the edge off, something to ground me.

Inside the suite, I pour myself a generous measure of whiskey, savoring the burn as it slides down my throat. The lights of the city stretch out beneath me, a glittering sea of possibilities and dangers. Somewhere out there, forces are already at work, conspiring to take what is rightfully Sophia's. And they wouldn't stop until they have it, or until they are dead.

My phone buzzes, pulling me from my thoughts. I glance at the screen and see Franco's name. I let it ring twice more before answering, taking another sip of whiskey as I walk over to the window.

"Angelo," Franco's voice comes through the line, calm and measured, but there is an underlying tension there that I knew all too well. "Did you find her?"

"I found her," I reply, keeping my voice even. "She's agreed to come back to New York."

There is a pause on the other end of the line, and I could almost hear Franco's mind working, weighing the implications of my words. "Did you tell her?"

I knew what he was asking, and the answer was simple. "No. Not yet."

"Angelo..." Franco's tone was careful, almost cautious. "She's your betrothed. She has a right to know."

"Not if telling her makes her run." I turn away from the window, pacing the length of the room. "You know as well as I do that if I told her the truth, she'd disappear before we could even get her on a plane. And if that happens, there's no telling what those bastards will do."

"But lying to her? Keeping something like this from her..."

"I'm not lying," I cut him off, my voice sharper than I intended. "I'm just not telling her everything. Not yet."

Another pause. Franco was never one to push too hard, but I could hear the doubt in his silence. "You really think it's wise to keep this from her?"

"Wise? No. Necessary? Yes." I rub a hand over my face, feeling the full weight of everything I'm carrying. "Look, I know how this sounds. But I need her to trust me first. If she thinks I'm just some asshole dragging her back into a life she doesn't want, she'll fight me every step of the way. I can't afford that right now. Neither can she."

"She's not going to trust you when she finds out you've been keeping this from her," Franco warns, his voice low. "And she will find out."

"I'll deal with that when the time comes," I say, dismissing the concern. "Right now, the priority is getting her back to New York safely. Everything else can wait."

Franco sighs, a sound that is more resigned than anything else. "Just be careful, Angelo. You know how dangerous this game is. And you're playing with more than just your life."

"I know," I say, and I mean it. Every word. "I'll be careful."

But as I end the call and set the phone down on the table, I can't shake the feeling that I'm already in too deep. Sophia is more than just a responsibility, more than just a pawn in this dangerous game we are playing. She is...important.

Important in a way I hadn't allowed anyone to be in a long time.

I down the rest of my whiskey, letting the burn chase away the thoughts I'm not ready to confront. There is no room for doubt here, no room for second-guessing. I have a job to do, and I will see it through. That's who I am. That is who I've always been.

But as I stare out at the city below, the lights twinkling like a thousand promises, I can't help but wonder if Sophia will forgive me when she learns the truth.

And if I would be able to forgive myself for the choices I was about to make.

Chapter Four

Sophia

The decision weighs on me like a thousand stones, each one carved from the fear of what I might be walking into. But fear isn't a luxury I can afford right now. Not when the people I care about are at risk.

I have lived my entire life trying to escape the shadow of my family's legacy, but now it seems that shadow has finally caught up to me, threatening to swallow everything I worked so hard to build.

I can't let that happen. Not to Justine and not to the small circle of friends who have become my makeshift family in London. And so, despite every instinct screaming at me to stay, to run, to do anything but this, I have made up my mind.

I'm going back to New York.

But it wasn't for me. It was for them. I had to keep them safe, and the only way to do that was to remove myself from the equation. If I stayed, they would always be in danger, always one step away from becoming collateral damage in a war that they knew nothing about.

My hands tremble slightly as I pack the last of my things into a suitcase. I haven't told Justine yet, and the thought of saying goodbye, of seeing the hurt in her eyes, makes my stomach twist with guilt. But this is the right choice. The only choice.

"Hey, Soph?" Justine's voice calls from the doorway, a bright contrast to the dark thoughts swirling in my mind. "Are you ready for our movie night? I've got all the snacks."

I pause, my back still turned to her as I zip up the suitcase. I want to avoid this moment, to somehow slip away without having to face the inevitable questions. But Justine deserves better than that. She has been my rock, my constant in a world that seems to shift beneath my feet at every turn.

Taking a deep breath, I turn to face her. Justine stood there, a wide smile on her face, holding up a bag of popcorn and a bottle of wine. Her smile falters when she notices the suitcase at my feet.

"What's going on, Sarah?" she asks, her voice laced with concern. "Why do you have a suitcase packed?"

I swallow hard, trying to find the right words. "I have to go back to New York, Justine."

The expression on her face shifts from concern to shock, then to something that looks like hurt. "Back to New York? What are you talking about? You hate New York."

"I know," I say, forcing myself to hold her gaze. "But it's something I have to do. It's not safe for me to stay here, and if I don't go...other people could get hurt."

Justine's eyes search mine, trying to understand. "What do you mean 'not safe'? Is this because of that man—Angelo?"

I nod slowly. "Yes. There are things happening that I didn't want you to be a part of, things I never told you about. But now...now I have no choice. I have to go back and deal with it, to keep you and everyone else safe."

Her lips press into a thin line, and I can see the wheels turning in her mind as she processes what I'm saying. "And you were just going to leave without telling me?"

I shake my head, feeling the weight of my guilt settle even deeper. "No, I was going to tell you. I just...didn't know how."

"Okay, then. When are we leaving?"

Her question startles me into looking up.

"J, you can't come with me."

"Like hell, I can't. You're my best friend, Sarah. You've been there for me through everything, and now you're telling me to just sit back and watch you go face whatever this is on your own? No way. I'm coming with you."

"No, you're not," I say, shaking my head vehemently.

"Remember those Tae Kwon Do lessons my mother made me take in primary? I remember them. Try and stop me."

I sigh, knowing that arguing with her was pointless.

"Fine, you can come with me."

She rolls her eyes and goes into the kitchen. "Try to sound a bit more excited love. I'm not marching you off to the executioners."

My smile is shaky. It isn't fair, letting her come with me when she still has no idea what we are going to face.

Telling Justine the truth is like trying to untangle a knot that has been tightened over the years—a knot made up of fear, secrets, and lies I'd told us both to keep her safe. But now, with everything unraveling, I have no choice but to cut through the layers and lay everything bare.

The flat is quiet, save for the soft hum of the kettle on the stove. I can hear Justine rummaging through the cupboards, her usual chatter filling the space as she searches for the tea bags.

"I swear, if you've moved those Earl Grey sachets again, we're going to have words," she calls out, her voice playful but with an edge that tells me she means it.

"They're in the second cupboard, behind the pasta," I reply, trying to keep my voice steady.

"Oh, thank God," she mutters, triumphantly holding up the box as she walks back into the living room.

"Honestly, I don't know how you function without a proper organizational system. It's a wonder you can find anything in this place."

I manage a small smile, but my heart is pounding in my chest. Justine sets the box down on the coffee table, eyeing me curiously as she pours hot water into two mugs.

"You've been quiet all morning," she says, her tone shifting from playful to concerned. "Is it because of New York? I know you're worried, but we'll figure it out."

I look down at my hands, the words I need to say tangling in my throat. "It's not just New York, Justine. There's…there's something I need to tell you."

She pauses, one eyebrow arching as she studies me. "Okay…I'm listening."

I take a deep breath, steeling myself for what I am about to reveal. "My name isn't Sarah Lacey. It never was."

The room seems to go still, the air thick with the weight of my confession. Justine doesn't say anything for a moment, she is just staring at me, her expression unreadable.

"Okay, I mean you had hinted that Sarah wasn't your real name back when we were kids," she finally says, her voice quiet.

I think of the "secret" that I shared with my new friend when we were little. I had immediately been terrified that my mother and I would be caught now that Justine knew. I had never explained anything else to her after that slip-up, too scared to confide more in her, too afraid that I had broken my mother's trust and put us in danger.

"My real name is Sophia Agostini," I continue, the words spilling out before I can second-guess myself. "My mother and I fled New York when I was a little girl. We changed our names, moved to England, and started over. She did it to protect me from my father's world—a world I never wanted to be a part of."

Justine blinks, processing what I've just told her. Then, to my surprise, she lets out a low whistle. "Well, shit. And here I thought you were going to tell me you secretly hated cats or something."

I can't help but laugh, even as the weight of the situation presses down on me. "No, I don't hate cats. But I am the daughter of a man who was deeply involved in the mafia. My mother took me away from all of that, and we've been in hiding ever since."

She leans back against the couch, crossing her arms over her chest. "Okay, so let me get this straight. You're not Sarah Lacey—you're Sophia Agostini. You're basically mafia royalty, and you've been hiding out here in London, pretending to be a regular old English girl?"

"Pretty much," I say, wincing at how absurd it sounds when she puts it like that.

"And now, Angelo—this hot, brooding guy with the world's most ridiculous cheekbones—has shown up and told you that your father is dead, and you have to go back to New York to...what? Take over the family business?"

I shake my head. "No, I don't want anything to do with the family business. But there's a power struggle happening back home, and because of who I am, I'm a target. If I don't go back, if I don't deal with this, then the people I care about could get caught in the crossfire."

Justine stares at me for a long moment. Then she sighs and runs a hand through her hair, shaking her head in disbelief. "Sophia Agostini, huh? You know, I always knew there was something you weren't telling me. I just didn't expect it to be...this."

"I'm sorry," I say quietly. "I didn't want to lie to you. I thought I was protecting you."

Her eyes soften, and she leans forward, resting her hand on mine. "I get that. But you have to understand how unfair it was to keep me in the dark like that. We've been through so much together, and it hurts to know you didn't trust me enough to tell me the truth."

"I do trust you," I insist, my voice thick with emotion. "But this...this is different. This is dangerous."

Justine's gaze doesn't waver, and when she speaks, her voice is firm. "I'm your best friend, Sarah, sorry...Sophia. This is weird."

I wince again and she shakes her head.

"I can handle the truth, no matter how messy or dangerous it is. What I can't handle is being treated like some delicate flower that needs to be protected from the big, bad world."

I nod, the guilt pressing down on me even harder. "You're right. I should have told you. I'm sorry."

She smiles, a small, genuine smile that makes my heart ache. "Apology accepted. Now, let's figure this out together, okay? I'm not letting you face this alone."

"Justine, you don't have to do this," I say, though I know it is pointless to argue. "This isn't your fight."

She rolls her eyes, her snarky humor slipping back into place. "Oh, please. You think I'm going to let you run off to New York with Mr. Mafia Hottie and not be there to see the drama unfold? I'd never forgive myself."

"Justine..." I start, but she cuts me off with a wave of her hand.

"Look, I know you're trying to protect me, but newsflash: I'm a big girl. I can make my own decisions. And right now, I'm deciding that I'm coming with you. End of discussion."

I sigh, knowing there is no winning this argument. Justine is as stubborn as they come, and once she makes up her mind, there is no changing it.

"Fine," I say, giving in. "But I'll have to go alone first. I need to make sure it's safe before you get involved."

She narrows her eyes, clearly not thrilled with the idea, but eventually nods. "Okay, but you'd better keep me updated. If I don't hear from you regularly, I'm getting on the next plane to New York and hunting you down."

"I will," I promise, feeling a strange mix of relief and anxiety at her determination. "Thank you, Justine. For everything."

She grins. "You're welcome. But don't think I'm letting you off the hook that easily. You owe me big time for this."

"I'll add it to the tab," I joke, the tension in the room finally easing.

"So," Justine says after a moment, a mischievous glint in her eyes, "how does it feel to be a mafia princess?"

I groan, burying my face in my hands. "Don't call me that."

She laughs, a bright, infectious sound that makes me smile despite everything. "Sorry, love. But you've got to admit, it's kind of badass."

I peek at her through my fingers, my own smile tugging at the corners of my mouth. "You're ridiculous, you know that?"

"Yep," she says, popping the "p" with a grin. "But you love me for it."

I did love her for it. Justine had a way of making even the heaviest situations feel lighter, of bringing humor and warmth into a world that often felt cold and unforgiving. She was the sister I'd never had, and I couldn't imagine going through this without her.

"Promise me something," I say, my voice more serious now. "Promise me you'll be careful. If things get too dangerous, I need to know you'll get out."

She meets my gaze, her expression softening. "I promise, Sarah...Sophia. But the same goes for you. Don't try to be a hero, okay? If things get too crazy, you get out. We'll figure it out together."

"Deal," I agree, feeling the knot of tension in my chest loosen just a bit.

***

Angelo is already seated across from me, his expression calm and unreadable. He has this unnerving ability to look completely at ease, even when the world is falling apart around him. Maybe it's the ridiculous glasses.

There's something completely disarming about the fact that he wears them. They should make him seem weak, but instead, it makes him seem even more powerful. And they act like a shield, somehow containing his emotions behind them, magnifying the green of his eyes but never revealing his innermost thoughts.

It's like he's always in control, always ten steps ahead of everyone else. I hate how much that rattles me.

"You made the right choice," Angelo says, breaking the silence.

I look up at him, trying to gauge his intentions. "Did I?"

He doesn't answer right away. He just watches me with those intensely green eyes of his. They remind me of the kind of eyes that are always given to the heroes in fantasy books. I nearly snort at my whimsical train of thought. I'm seated across from a mafia don and I'm comparing his pretty eyes to the heroes in the fairy smut I like to read.

"You're doing this to protect the people you care about. That's the right choice," he was saying. I tug my attention back to the present.

I nod, though I don't feel any less conflicted. "So, what's the plan when we get there?"

Angelo leans back in his seat, his gaze still fixed on me. "For your safety, we'll need to keep up appearances. It'll be easier to navigate this world if people believe we're engaged."

The statement hangs in the air between us, and I can't help but frown. "Engaged? Why would they believe that?"

He shrugs, as if it was the most natural thing in the world. "Because it makes sense. We were betrothed when you were a child. And in this world, old promises still carry weight. If people think we're together, they'll be less likely to try anything."

I narrow my eyes, skepticism creeping in. "And what if I say no? What if I don't want to play this game?"

His lips curve into a small, almost teasing smile. "It's just another game of pretend, Sophia. You're good at those, aren't you?"

The way he says the words makes my skin prickle, like he knows more about me than he should, like he can see right through the facade I have worked so hard to build. And maybe he can. Angelo Castiglia isn't the kind of man you can easily deceive.

But he's right. Pretending was something I had grown up doing. Pretending to be someone else, pretending to be fine, pretending that the life I had left behind didn't haunt me. This would be no different. At least, that's what I tried to tell myself.

I sigh, looking out the window as the plane lifts off the ground, leaving London—and my old life—behind. "Fine. I'll play along. But don't expect me to be happy about it."

"I wouldn't dream of it," Angelo replies smoothly, his tone full of amusement.

I don't look at him. I don't want to see the satisfaction in his eyes. I can already feel the walls closing in, the weight of the decision I have made pressing down on me. But it's too late to turn back now. I'm committed to this path, whether I like it or not.

As the plane soars higher into the sky, I can't shake the feeling that I'm stepping into a trap, one that was carefully laid out long before I ever knew it existed.

And the worst part is, I had no idea who was really pulling the strings.

Chapter Five

Angelo

Earlier That Day

The streets of London blur into a gray haze as the car weaves through the city, making its way to Sophia's flat. The rain has slowed to a drizzle, barely more than a mist, but it still clings to the air, making everything feel cold and damp. I lean back in my seat, staring out the window, my mind already on Sophia and what lies ahead.

I shouldn't be this restless. Picking her up, escorting her to the car—it was all standard procedure. And yet, there was an undercurrent of anticipation in me that I hadn't felt in years, a low hum just beneath my skin that made my fingers twitch and my thoughts stray.

She had gotten under my skin. From the moment I saw her at the funeral, she had gotten under my skin. That fire in her eyes, the defiance she wore like designer perfume—it was a challenge, one I hadn't been able to ignore. And now, as I prepared to bring her back to New York, that challenge was front and center in my mind.

It wasn't just about her safety. It wasn't just about fulfilling a duty or protecting an heir.

It was about her—Sophia, her beauty, which was almost ridiculous, her voice which offered that raspy, sultry goodness I've always liked. I've had dreams of that voice, but in those dreams, she's not arguing with me. In those dreams, she's screaming my name, begging me to fuck her harder.

Fuck.

I can feel myself getting hard just thinking about it, which is unfortunate because the Audi is pulling up at her building. I can only imagine the look on her face if I were to show up on her doorstep with a raging hard-on. I run my tongue across my teeth and try not to commit an act of indecency on the proper, posh streets of London.

But it isn't just the absurd physical attraction I feel for her. That I could deal with easily. No, it was everything else that drew me to her. It was all her complexities and contradictions.

Her vulnerability was wrapped up in cement and gravel, forming an impenetrable wall I wanted to breach.

It was the way she looked at me, like she was daring me to break down those walls, but at the same time, so clearly desperate to keep them up.

We pull up in front of her building, the car coming to a smooth stop. I glance at the driver, nodding once before stepping out into the misty air. The dampness settles on my coat, but I barely notice as I cross the sidewalk to the entrance of her building.

We agreed to meet here by two, but she isn't on her doorstep like I expected her to be. And so, I press the doorbell. The door flies open with a vengeance and then she's there, staring at me, her face pale but no less beautiful.

The last time Sophia was in my presence, she'd been wrapped up in beautiful black clothes, her hair tied in a knot at the back of her head, conservative makeup, no jewelry. She'd been a picture of elegance and collection. Someone had clearly made a switch when I wasn't looking, however, because the woman standing in front of me was the embodiment of chaos.

Her hair is unbound and all over the place in a half-frizzy mess. It looks like it had once upon a time been a ponytail, but the elastic band is hanging off the ends of her hair by literal strands. She's wearing shorts, very short shorts. I can't stop myself from looking down at her tan thighs.

Even if there was a gun trained on my head, I don't think I could have prevented myself from staring. The tank top she has on does nothing to hide the hard points of her nipples and...shit, they are definitely not helping the situation.

"What the hell are you doing here?"

I blink and turn to look behind me. Perhaps someone else had sprouted out of the bushes, and she's talking to them.

"Picking you up."

"We agreed to meet at two."

I pull out my phone from my pocket and show it to her. It's two minutes past two.

"Shit. Sorry, oh gosh, I...was packing and I got carried away with sorting out my mother's belongings and...you probably don't care about any of that."

I just stand there staring at her, literally unable to form words.

"I suppose I should invite you in." She steps aside, and I enter the flat.

Sophia's flat is a study in contradictions. The space is neat—almost too neat—with minimal furniture and few personal touches. It's clear that she lives with just the essentials on hand—as if she can pack up and leave at a moment's notice. Yet, there are signs of recent chaos, traces of a life with more depth than you can see at first glance.

A small stack of boxes sits in the corner, half-filled with what look like her mother's belongings: old photo albums, worn books, and delicate trinkets that seem out of place in an otherwise unadorned room.

The kitchen table is cluttered with papers and a half-empty mug of tea, signs of a woman trying to sort through memories she isn't ready to leave behind.

A well-worn sofa, the only piece of furniture that seems lived in, faces a window where a single plant struggles for sunlight. The scent of lavender lingers in the air, a small touch of warmth in a space that feels more like a temporary shelter than a home.

"I just have to grab a few more things and we can be on our way. Drink?"

"Water, thank you."

She opens her fridge and bends to retrieve a bottle of water, giving me a full view of her ass.

"How long have you lived here?" I ask because it's not what I had expected. I expected numerous boxes with treasures and memories, not a few cardboard boxes with pans and old broken things in them.

"Four years, give or take. Why? Not glamorous enough for you?" she says sharply.

I keep my eyes trained on her as I gulp the water down and I see her throat bob as she watches me. Her eyes go languid, losing some of their trained hardness, and I see goosebumps rise on her exposed skin. Good.

"Not glamorous enough for anybody, especially not my fiancé."

"Putting in the practice for New York, are you?"

I decide that her voice really is my addiction. I love the tinge of an English accent, coupled with her Italian vowels. It makes me feel light-headed.

"You should get used to it."

She sighs and turns away from me, which is good because I was beginning to think ridiculous thoughts like that I should pin her against the fridge and find out if her body is as soft as it looks.

She moves through the flat with practiced efficiency, gathering the last of her things, but there is a tension in her movements—a reluctance to fully let go.

She comes back into the kitchen wearing a dress. It's form-fitting and beautiful, and it makes me want to smile.

"Can't arrive in New York looking like something the cat dragged in, now can I?"

"No. You look beautiful."

That seems to startle her into a rare moment of silence, her mouth hanging open and her breathing quick. And we stand there for what must be only seconds, but it feels far longer, just staring at each other.

She is used to running, to being ready to disappear, but this time, it isn't just another escape. This is different, and I can see it in the way she pauses to glance at her mother's things, a fleeting moment of hesitation before she turns to face me.

"Is this everything?" I ask quietly, breaking whatever the hell is gathering between us.

She nods, but her eyes linger on the room for just a second longer, as if saying goodbye to the life she has built here—the life she is about to leave behind.

"Ready?" I ask, my voice low. It sounds almost intimate in the quiet of the entranceway, and my heart leaps a little. She must feel the tension between us too, because her eyes lock on mine for a moment, something warm glowing in their depths. Then she turns away, and the spell is broken.

She nods, her fingers tightening around the handle of her suitcase. "Ready as I'll ever be."

I reach for her suitcase, our fingers brushing as I take it from her. The contact is brief, but it is enough to send a spark of awareness shooting through me, straight to my core. I can feel the warmth of her skin even after I let go, the sensation lingering like a phantom touch.

"Allow me."

She doesn't argue, but I can see the tension in her frame, the way she is trying to hold herself together. I admire that about her—the strength, the resolve—but I also want to see what is beneath it. I want to know what it would take to make her drop that guard, to see her for who she really is.

I lead the way back to the car, my hand resting lightly on the small of her back and my fingers twitching like I'm a fucking schoolboy touching a girl for the first time.

It's a casual touch, nothing more than a gesture of guidance, but the instant my palm makes contact with her body, I feel a subtle shiver run through her body. She doesn't pull away, but I can sense the way she tenses, the way her breath hitches slightly, as if she's trying to maintain control.

Good. I want her to feel this. I want her to be as aware of me, as I am of her.

As we reach the car, I open the door and gesture for her to get in. She hesitates for just a moment, her eyes meeting mine, and I can see the conflict there.

"Remember, it's just a game, Sophia,"

Her lips press into a thin line, but she doesn't argue. Instead, she slides into the backseat, her movements graceful and controlled. I follow her in, closing the door behind me as the car pulls away from the curb.

The silence between us is thick, charged with an energy that neither of us can ignore. I can feel her beside me, the heat of her body just inches away, the soft scent of her perfume lingering in the air.

Every part of me is hyper-aware of her—of the way she shifts slightly in her seat, the way her fingers curl into the fabric of her coat, the way her chest rises and falls with each measured breath.

I want to touch her again. I want to feel that spark, that connection. I want to see if it is as electric as it was the first time. But I hold back, letting the tension build, letting her feel the weight of it.

"Why are you doing this?" she asks suddenly, her voice breaking the silence. There is a vulnerability in her tone, a crack in the armor she wears so carefully.

"Doing what?" I reply, my voice calm, even as the intensity between us threatens to boil over.

"This." She gestures between us, her brow furrowing slightly. "This whole...act. Pretending to be engaged, pretending to care about what happens to me. What's in it for you?"

I consider her question, knowing that the answer is more complicated than she realizes. There are so many layers to this, to us. Layers that I'm not ready to peel back just yet.

"You're an asset of sorts. Having you dead would be really bad for business,"

She snorts loudly. "Good to know that's all I am to you."

She doesn't look at me, and I don't look at her either.

"I didn't take you as someone who liked or wanted empty words."

"That's good, because I'm not."

"I also made a promise to your father."

She scoffs again and turns to face me.

"My father didn't give two shits about me. He was a sadistic, awful man and I'm happy my mom took me away when she did."

It really isn't my business what she thinks or how she feels, at least it shouldn't be, but I can't stand the pain behind her cold words.

"Carlo Agostini was the most powerful man in the Cosa Nostra. He excelled in finding people. Do you think he couldn't find you? He could've come and dragged you back to New York to live under his reign of terror, but he didn't. Make of that what you will."

She sighs, closing her eyes. "I suppose I knew that," she admits. "But I always figured that he just didn't care. Part of me imagined that he must have another heir, a son. Maybe he remarried and that was why he didn't come looking for me. It was a relief…and an insult."

Her words are raw and I feel a pang, at the pain I can hear in them. Her life has been complicated, strange, full of lies and deceit, yet she still wants to know that her father loved her. Maybe none of us is exempt from wishing for the fealty and support of our parents.

"If it's any consolation," I say to her, "he never remarried, and he never stopped talking about you. He never mentioned your mother, but he always spoke of you with pride.

Her eyes snap open and she looks at me closely. "He had people watching me," she says perceptively, and I look down, uncomfortable under the intensity of her gaze. She has hit upon one of the things that I didn't want to reveal to her just yet. It was how I knew where she was. It was how I knew her mother had died.

I finally lift my eyes to meet hers. "Yes," I say honestly. "It's how I knew where you were and how to find you. He told me to go to you when he knew he was dying. He was afraid for you."

Her face is tight, but I can see the conflict warring within her. I reach out and pick up her hand, giving it a squeeze. "I know it's not easy, and you have every right to be angry, but he did love you."

She squeezes my fingers back, and looked away, but not before I see a tear slip down her cheek. I look at our joined hands, and my cock throbs, even as my heart hurts for her. I ponder the mixture of emotions that she is making me feel.

I want her. I have wanted her from the moment I saw her, and now, as I feel her respond to my touch, that desire burns hotter and more fiercely than ever.

But this isn't just about desire. This is about trust. About getting her to let go, to open up, to see that I'm not the enemy.

I can't rush it. I have to let her come to me, let her make the choice. Because when she does—when she finally lets those walls come down—it will be all the more satisfying.

"I'm not your enemy," I say, my voice a low rumble. "You know that, don't you?"

Her eyes flutter open, and she looks at me, really looks at me, as if she is seeing me for the first time. The conflict in her gaze is still there, but so is something else—something that makes my heart pound and my blood sing.

"Maybe," she whispers, her voice barely audible.

The rest of the ride passes in a charged silence, the air between us thick with unspoken tension. But I can feel the shift, the slow, inevitable pull that is drawing us closer together. She can fight it, resist it, but I know that sooner or later, she will give in.

And when she does, there will be no turning back.

Chapter Six

SOPHIA

This plane is a far cry from the commercial flights I have taken in the past. Angelo's private jet is luxurious. It offers the kind of opulence that makes it hard to forget who I'm dealing with. The seats are plush, the lighting soft, and the air feels crisp, like it's somehow fresher than the air outside.

The plane's engines hum softly, a steady vibration that thrums through the plush seats. It's the only sound breaking the thick silence between Angelo and me. Outside, the night sky is an endless expanse of darkness, the clouds below us like a blanket of uncertainty.

And then there is Angelo. Sitting across from me, his presence is impossible to ignore. He is calm, almost too calm, as if he is completely at ease with the situation. But I'm not fooled. I can feel the tension in the air, thick and heavy, like a storm waiting to break. It isn't just the situation that has me on edge—it's him.

Every time I look at him, I feel a pull, something magnetic that makes it hard to think straight. It's infuriating, how he manages to get under my skin without even trying, how he can make my heart race with just a glance.

I hate it, hate that he has this power over me. But there is no denying the chemistry between us, the way my body reacts to him, even when my mind screams at me to keep my distance.

As if sensing my thoughts, Angelo shifts in his seat, his gaze sliding over to me. His eyes are bright and intense. It's the kind of look that makes it hard to breathe. I try to ignore it, try to focus on anything else, but it's impossible.

The air between us is charged, crackling with unspoken tension, and I can feel it pulling us closer together, drawing me into his orbit.

"Stop looking at me like that." I probably sound like a petulant child, but I can't help it.

"Like what?" His voice is low and inviting. I feel it in my core as it washes over me. I can't help it that I'm clenching my thighs together, and I release a shaky breath as his eyes follow the movement of my legs.

"Like what, Sophia?" he says again.

I swallow, already feeling my nipples tightening to hard buds. Maybe it hadn't been the brightest idea to wear my flimsiest lace bra when I knew how much he affected me, or maybe a part of me had wanted to be ready for...for what?

What's that thing Justine always says? When in doubt, go for hard, unfiltered honesty.

"Like you're thinking about fucking me."

Something shifts in his gaze. His eyes narrow slightly, as if he has been waiting for those words. He stands, his movements fluid and deliberate, and he crosses the small space between us. I watch him, my breath catching in my throat as he reaches out, his hand brushing against my arm, sending a shiver down my spine.

"And if I am?"

My heart pounds in my chest, every rational thought slipping away as his fingers trace a line down my arm, his touch light but electrifying. I look up at him, meeting his gaze, and for a moment, everything else falls away—the fear, the uncertainty, the questions.

All that is left is him, and the way he makes me feel.

"I should tell you to fuck right off."

That makes him smile.

"Will you?"

I shake my head.

"Good," he replies, his voice a low rumble. "Because I've been waiting for this."

My breath hitches, every nerve in my body on fire as his lips brush against mine. The touch is so light it's almost maddening. I can feel the heat radiating from him, and the tension coils tighter within me, ready to snap.

And then, in one swift movement, he closes the distance between us, his lips capturing mine in a kiss that is anything but gentle. It's fierce, hungry, filled with all the pent-up desire we have been trying so hard to ignore.

I gasp against his mouth, my hands gripping his shirt as I kiss him back, all thoughts of resistance melting away.

He pulls me closer, his hands roaming over my body, exploring, claiming. I can feel his heartbeat against mine, the steady rhythm mirroring the rapid pace of my own. Everything else fades into the background.

There is only this, only him, and the way he makes me burn.

"Angelo," I breathe, my voice full of desperation.

"Say that again."

He sounds crazed, his fingers already slipping underneath the hem of my dress, teasing me as they progress toward my aching core.

"Angelo." It doesn't even sound like my voice speaking his name. I sound like a woman in a porn video. I feel a sharper throb of want in my pussy.

"Fuck, I've dreamed of you calling out to me, just like this, but in my dreams. You're naked and draped over my lap, and my handprint is on your ass."

I was wet before, but his words turn on the waterworks for real. I feel his fingers sliding through my wetness and he growls approvingly.

"What are you waiting for, then?"

He doesn't need any more encouragement before he's yanking the dress over my head and tossing it to the floor. His calloused palm slides down my throat and into the valley between my lace-clad breasts.

"Fucking perfect. I knew they would be."

He palms a breast, twisting and turning the nipple between his thumb and forefinger and I throw my head back in ecstasy. He deftly removes my bra so that he can attend to both of my breasts, licking, biting, sucking.

"Don't stop," I beg, holding on to fistfuls of his thick hair.

He lifts me off my seat and my breasts bounce perkily as I settle onto my feet again. I can hear myself panting, the sound filling the space between us as I stare at him, captured by his smoky green eyes. I think again of the fairy smut I have been reading and I want to cackle with delight. This is so much better than any book.

It's almost obscene, standing before him wearing just my lacy thong and my arousal while he is still fully dressed.

"You're breaking the rules of the game Angelo."

"And what are the rules? *Tesoro mio*?"

As he speaks the words, he casts his jacket onto the seat behind him and starts taking off his tie. I swallow hard as I watch him revealing himself a little bit at a time. He unbuttons the top two buttons of his shirt, but then he stops. He gives me a smile, and my heart flips over in my chest. We just stare at each other for a moment. I squirm, desperate for him, desperate for his touch.

"Clothes off," I finally say to him.

"Take them off yourself, *Tesoro mio.*"

Gladly.

I begin unbuttoning his shirt, but my fingers are trembling so much that he takes over. I bend forward to run my tongue down his torso, and he groans.

"I like that a little too much."

I bite on his nipple next, and I am rewarded with his shocked hiss.

"There should be rules about this," I say against his skin. "We should have boundaries."

He chuckles, and I can feel the sound through my lips. I tilt my head back to look up at him, at his too-handsome face, at his full lips, at the sultry heat in his eyes.

"Rules are made to be broken," he whispers as he slips two fingers inside of me.

"Oh fuck." I hold on to him for dear life as he curves his fingers, hitting that sweet, mythical spot that most men can't ever find. I cry out as waves upon waves of pleasure wash over me.

My orgasm crashes into me so suddenly that I fall against him, a sopping, shaking mess.

"Oh my God," I pant, clinging to his bare arms, my face pressed against his smooth chest. "Oh my God."

"You look beautiful when you come," he says huskily. He sets me away from him for a moment so that he can take off his pants. I blink a little as he turns to face me again, taking in the size of him. He's huge, but he's perfect.

I abruptly remember Justine talking about a guy she was hooking up with who had "the prettiest penis" she had ever seen. I remember laughing at her, because how could a penis be "pretty"? However, looking at Angelo, I suddenly understood what she meant. He's beautiful from head to toe, utterly perfect in every way.

"My turn," I announce, dropping to my knees and wrapping my hands around his length. I suck him into my mouth with an eagerness that surprises even me.

"Sophia...fuck!"

My tongue works over his skin as I fist the length of him and tug gently. I start to take him deeper, but he pulls me gently away.

"This is very generous of you, but this is not what I want right now." He looks down at me, his chest rising and falling.

"What do you want, then?" I ask, licking my lips.

He says something in Italian that I don't understand, but the words are musical and beautiful in my ears. He pulls me to my feet, turning to take a seat. He tugs me onto his lap, and in one fluid, mind-numbing stroke, he buries himself inside me.

We sigh in unison, and I move against him, unable to hold still. He's big, and there's a bit of pain, but the pleasure is already overcoming the little prickles of discomfort at taking him in one stroke.

"Fuck, I knew it would be like this," he says his hands lifting my hair off my shoulders. I feel his cock twitch inside of me.

"Like what?"

"Perfect. Fucking perfect."

Something inside of me cracks open, like the lid coming off a jar that has been sealed too tight for a long time. I swoop down to kiss his lips, and he starts moving inside of me. We quickly find a cadence together, as if we have been doing this for years.

"Angelo," I gasp, tipping my head back as my orgasm looms. "I'm going to come."

"Do it," he orders me, his voice sharp. His long fingers come to rest on my clit just as he slaps my ass hard with the other hand. "Come for me, *Tesoro mio.*"

As if my body was waiting for his command, I shatter, screaming his name as I tremble against him. I cling to him as I see stars, dying and being born again, a changed person. I had no idea sex could be like this. I have never experienced anything that approaches it in all of my life.

Angelo murmurs something approving in Italian, and strokes into me two more times before coming, his fingers tangled in my hair, tugging until it hurts, his cheek pressed between my breasts.

We stay still for a moment, both gasping for air, both sticky with sweat and our mingled pleasure.

"That was..." I start to say, but stop. I have no words for what I just experienced.

"Incredible," he says simply, pressing a warm kiss to the spot between my breasts. "You are incredible, *Tesoro mio.*"

"What does that mean?" I ask, shifting a little as my foot cramps up.

"My darling, or my treasure," he replies, helping me to lift myself off him.

I'm not sure what to make of that. We barely know one another, but then again, what we just shared changes everything. I don't know if I want to be his darling, but I like the way the endearment sounds falling off his lips.

"Don't overthink it," he suggests, tweaking my nose playfully. "The sex was good. Leave it at that."

I smirk at him. "Good" doesn't even begin to cover it. I still feel weak in the knees and my body keeps clenching with little aftershocks of pleasure.

"Come on," he says, taking my hand. "Let's get cleaned up and dressed. I'm sure the flight crew is tired of hiding out."

I feel a flush rush over my skin. I had completely forgotten where we were and what we were doing. I look around, horrified, and scoop up my clothing from the floor. I notice with renewed horror that there's a wet spot on the chair where we fucked.

Angelo starts laughing, the sound bright and carefree, and I feel my worries dissolve a little. "Don't panic. They won't talk about this," he assures me. He leans over to whisper in my ear. "Besides, I've always wanted to join the mile-high club."

I giggle in spite of my embarrassment and follow him toward the bathroom at the back of the plane to get cleaned up.

Chapter Seven

Sophia

The plane lands with a soft thud, jolting me awake. As I blink away the remnants of sleep, the reality of where I am hits me like a freight train. New York. The city that has witnessed both my earliest, sweetest memories and the darkest days of my life.

Angelo is quiet beside me, his presence a steady reminder of why I'm here, of what lies ahead. I glance at him out of the corner of my eye—calm, collected, like this is just another day for him. But for me, it's anything but.

As the plane taxies to a stop, I can't help the flood of memories that surge forward, memories of a time when New York was my entire world.

I used to run through the lush grass of Central Park, my tiny legs struggling to keep up with my papa's long strides.

I could still hear my mama's laughter, light and carefree, as she called me back to her side. We'd stop for ice cream at the corner cart, the sweet, sticky treat dripping down my fingers as I tried to eat it faster than it melted. And then there was the pizza—with pepperoni and sausage, my absolute favorite, back when the world seemed like a place that only shat up rainbows and unicorns.

But those were fading memories, dulled by time and overshadowed by the last day I spent in this city. The day everything changed.

I remembered that day vividly—the frantic packing, the hushed conversations between my mother and her maid, the fear in my mother's eyes that she tried so hard to hide from me. We were going on a "trip", she'd said, but even at seven years old, I knew something wasn't right.

Paris was supposed to be the City of Light, but it became the city where everything I knew was extinguished. The city where I learned that fairy tales weren't real and monsters were all too real.

Now, as the plane door opened, letting in a rush of cool morning air, those memories felt like a lifetime ago. I wasn't that innocent little girl anymore, and New York wasn't the safe haven it once was.

"We're here," Angelo says unnecessarily, pulling me back to the present.

"I noticed," I reply, my voice tight. I want to say more, to find some way to explain the turmoil inside me, but what's the point? Angelo isn't here to play therapist and I'm not about to bare my soul to him.

He turns to me, his green eyes steady. I feel a pang at the lack of emotion in them. He's back to business then. I miss the charming lover who made jokes and called me Italian endearments "Ready?"

"Are you always this chipper after a long flight?" I shoot back, hoping to lighten the mood—or at least distract myself from the memories clawing at my insides.

A faint smirk tugs at the corner of his mouth. "Only when I'm returning home with beautiful company."

I roll my eyes, but there's no denying the flutter in my chest at his words. "How sweet. I'm sure all your 'beautiful' guests appreciate your warm welcome."

"None of them have complained yet. You didn't seem to mind when my tongue was down your throat, and my fingers were..."

"Okay, you can stop now. What happens in the mile-high club stays in the mile-high club."

"If you say so," he says to me, offering his arm.

I hesitate before taking it. The moment our fingers touch, that familiar spark shoots through me, making it hard to think straight. I hate how easily he can make me feel this way—vulnerable, exposed and completely aware of him.

As we descend the steps and step onto the tarmac, I feel the weight of the city settle over me. The skyline looms in the distance, and for a moment, I'm that little girl again, running through the streets with nothing but joy and endless possibilities ahead of her. But those days are gone, replaced by the harsh reality of what New York has become for me.

The car waiting for us is sleek and black, a symbol of the power and influence that Angelo wields so effortlessly. The driver opens the door and I slide into the backseat, feeling the weight of what is to come pressing down on me.

We ride in silence, but it's not a comfortable silence. It's thick with unspoken words, questions I'm not ready to ask, and answers Angelo isn't willing to give. I can feel his eyes on me, like he's waiting for me to say something, to crack under the pressure. But I'm not about to give him the satisfaction.

Finally, I break the silence. "So, what's the plan? Do I get a bulletproof vest and a personal bodyguard? Or are you just going to lock me in your penthouse and throw away the key?"

He turns to me, one eyebrow raised. "I thought you'd enjoy living in a penthouse with security. It will save you from having to run away again"

I clench my jaw, refusing to rise to the bait. "I'm not running. I'm...strategically retreating."

"Whatever helps you sleep at night, *Tesoro mio*."

His use of the endearment sends a shiver down my spine, but I force myself to focus. "So, what's next? Am I supposed to just wait around until you decide what to do with me?"

"Something like that," he replies casually, like we're discussing dinner plans and not my future. "First, you get settled in. Then, we figure out who's after you and how to keep you safe."

I scoff. "And what if I don't want your protection?"

He leans in closer, his voice dropping to a low murmur. "You don't have a choice, Sophia. You're here now and that means you're under my care. Whether you like it or not."

The intensity in his gaze makes my heart race, and I hate how much it affects me. "Fine," I mutter, turning away to look out the window. The city whizzes by in a blur of light and shadow, a stark reminder of everything I have lost—and everything I am about to face.

We pull up in front of a towering glass building, the kind that screams wealth and power. The doorman nods at us as we walk in, and I follow Angelo to the elevator, feeling the weight of his presence beside me.

The ride up to the penthouse is quiet, but the tension between us crackles like electricity. When the doors finally slide open, revealing the luxurious apartment that will be my new prison, I step inside, taking in the sleek furniture, the polished floors, and the floor-to-ceiling windows that offer a breathtaking view of the city below.

"This is it," Angelo says, his voice steady.

I nod, trying to ignore the knot of anxiety tightening in my chest. "It's nice. If you're into cold, impersonal spaces."

He smirks. "I thought you'd appreciate the lack of personal touches. Makes it easier to leave when you're ready to run again."

I shot him a glare, but his words hit too close to home. "You don't know me, Angelo. Stop picking at me."

"I don't know you?" He steps closer, his gaze piercing. "You've been running your whole life, Sophia. But you can't run from this. I need you to understand that."

I want to argue, to tell him he's wrong, but the truth is, I wasn't sure he was. The past had finally caught up with me, and now, there was no escaping it. No more running, no more hiding.

"Get some rest," he says, his tone softening slightly. "You'll need it."

I nod, though the idea of rest feels impossible with the storm of emotions swirling inside me. I turn to look out at the city, the skyline shimmering in the early morning light. It's beautiful, but it feels like a mirage—something out of reach, something I can't hold on to.

Behind me, I feel Angelo's presence, warm and steady, a contrast to the icy fear that has settled in my chest.

"Sophia," he says, his voice low and reassuring. "We'll get through this. Together."

His words, simple as they were, offer a small measure of comfort to me. I nod, not trusting myself to speak.

Angelo reaches out, his hand brushing against mine, the touch sending that familiar shiver down my spine. It's a reminder of everything that has happened between us and everything that is still to come.

"Rest," he repeats, his voice a gentle command.

I nod again, my throat tight with emotions I can't name. As I turn to head toward the bedroom, I feel his gaze linger on me, a weight that is both comforting and unsettling.

This is only the beginning. Whatever comes next, I know it will be a test of everything—my strength, my resolve, and my heart.

And I'm not sure I'm ready for any of it.

Chapter Eight

Angelo

The penthouse is quiet, the only sound the soft click of the door as Sophia disappears into her bedroom. I watch her go, my eyes lingering on the spot where she just stood, the echo of her presence still vibrating in the air.

She's like a storm, that woman—fierce, unpredictable, and impossible to ignore. No matter how hard I try to keep my focus on the task at hand, she has a way of pulling me in, dragging me into the eye of the hurricane she carries with her.

And I'm being dragged willingly, aren't I?

The thought makes me scowl as I turn away from the bedroom door. It's dangerous, this pull I feel toward her. Dangerous for me, dangerous for her, and dangerous for the plan. But no matter how many times I remind myself of that, I can't shake the feeling that I'm standing on the edge of something I can't control.

It doesn't help that I can still taste her on my tongue, I can still feel her skin on mine, the hard pull of her fingers in my hair. I can still see her eyes shrouded in desire. Fuck, I could still hear her screaming my name as she came for the second time, quivering and holding onto me for dear life.

I was an idiot to think once with her would be enough. It was the classic case of an addict saying, "just one more time, and then I'll quit".

I walk to the massive windows that line the far wall of the living room, the city sprawling out beneath me in a glittering web of lights and shadows. New York is a city of contrasts, a place where power and vulnerability coexist in a precarious balance. It's a place that has given me everything, and taken away just as much.

And now, I'm bringing Sophia into it, into this world of power plays and hidden dangers. She is strong—stronger than she knows—but this world has a way of breaking even the toughest of us. It broke me once, and I wasn't sure I had the strength to keep her from the same fate.

But I will try. For her, I will try.

A low buzz from my phone snaps me out of my thoughts. I pull it from my pocket, glancing at the screen.

Franco's name flashes across it, a reminder that there is still work to be done, still threats lurking in the shadows.

"Franco," I greet him, keeping my voice low. "We're back."

"Good," he replies, his tone clipped. "Is she settled?"

"She's okay," I say, glancing back at the closed door. "Trying to get some rest."

"Rest might be hard to come by for any of us for a while," Franco says, his voice tight. "We've got movement on our end. Costa's men have been spotted in the city. They're looking for her."

A surge of anger rises in me, cold and sharp. Giuseppe Costa has been a thorn in my side for years, always lurking in the background, waiting for his moment to strike. And now, with Sophia back in the picture, he clearly saw an opportunity.

"He's not getting anywhere near her," I say, my voice hard as steel. "We'll deal with him."

Franco is silent for a moment, and I can almost hear the gears turning in his mind. "And what about Sophia? Does she know about what the betrothal means?"

The question hangs in the air between us, a weight I'm not ready to lift. "No," I admit, my jaw tightening. "Not yet."

"Angelo," Franco's voice is heavy with a note of warning. "You can't keep this from her forever. She's going to find out."

"I know," I reply, turning back to the window, the city below reflecting my inner turmoil. "But telling her now won't help. She's already on edge, already suspicious. If I drop this on her, she'll run."

"Or she'll fight," Franco counters. "She's stronger than you give her credit for."

I knew that. God, I knew that better than anyone. But I also knew that Sophia was unpredictable, a wild card in a game that required precision and control. If she found out about the real terms of the betrothal now, before I had a chance to earn her trust, it could blow everything up.

"I'll tell her when the time is right," I say, more to convince myself than Franco. "But not yet."

There is a pause on the other end of the call, and I can sense Franco weighing his next words carefully. "Just be careful, Angelo. You've got a lot riding on this. And so does she. And so do I, frankly."

I knew that. I knew what the sting of betrayal felt like, and I knew that people like us didn't forgive it. This is no act. She will be getting married to me, whether she wants to or not. Her safety depended upon it.

But it makes me feel like shit to have to lie to her, especially when she has lived her entire life being lied to. Her father lied, her mother lied to her for twenty years, and here I was doing the exact same thing. Really living up to that reputation. My own father would be proud.

Thinking of my old man made me grimace. Sophia might hate her own father, but she has no idea how bad things could have been. It was a blessing that her father allowed her to remain in hiding, didn't pressure her to come back to take her place as his daughter.

My own childhood was like something from a nightmare. I wouldn't have wished such an experience on anyone else. It had made me into the perfect soldier for my father, for my family, but it had been torture at times.

"I will remember that," I promise, ending the call before I say too much.

I slip the phone back into my pocket, my mind still racing. The betrothal is a complication, one I have been trying to navigate since the moment I found Sophia. It's the key to everything—her safety, her place in this world, and my control over the situation. But it's also a ticking time bomb, one that might explode if I'm not careful.

But it's not just the betrothal that worries me. It's Sophia herself. The way she challenges me, pushes me, makes me question everything I think I know. It's the way she makes me want things I haven't allowed myself to want in years.

I have to stay focused, have to keep my eye on the goal. But with Sophia, focus is becoming hard to maintain. She's a distraction, a dangerous one, but one I can't seem to stay away from.

I walk back to the bar in the corner of the living room, pouring myself a glass of whiskey. The amber liquid swirls in the glass, catching the light as I bring it to my lips. The burn is familiar and comforting, but it does little to quiet the turmoil inside me.

I'm a man who thrives on control, who has built his life on power and influence. But with Sophia, control is slipping through my fingers like sand. And the more I try to hold on, the faster it seems to slip away.

But I can't let her see that. She needs to believe that I'm in control, that I have everything under control. Because if she doesn't, if she sees through the cracks, she'll run. And that's something I can't afford to let happen.

Not now. Not ever.

As I down the last of the whiskey, I hear the bedroom door creak open. I turn, catching sight of Sophia as she steps out, her hair tousled from sleep, her eyes still heavy with exhaustion.

But even in her disheveled state, she's beautiful. Too beautiful for her own good.

"Can't sleep?" I ask, keeping my tone casual, though the sight of her makes my pulse quicken.

She shakes her head, her eyes meeting mine with a mixture of weariness and something else—something that makes my chest tighten. "Too much on my mind."

"Want to talk about it?" I offer, though I'm not sure if I want to hear what she has to say. Her thoughts, her feelings—they're a minefield. One wrong step, and everything could blow up in my face.

"Getting sentimental, are we?" She rolls her eyes and perches on the coffee table beside me. It's a piece of furniture that certainly isn't meant to be used as a chair.

"I see places aren't the only things you run away from." My comment makes her bristle, and I would smile, but I think I might get castrated.

"You're not wrong." Her sigh is soft. "But there's nothing to talk about. I'm just...trying to figure out how I got here. How everything got so messed up."

I want to tell her that she isn't alone, that I'm trying to figure it out too. But instead, I stay silent, letting her have this moment. I can see the weight of everything pressing down on her, the way her shoulders sag under the burden of it all.

She's strong, but even the strongest people need someone to lean on from time to time.

"Whatever it is, we'll get through it," I say, my voice firm, hoping to offer her some semblance of reassurance. "Together."

She glances at me, her eyes searching mine, and for a moment, I think she might say something—something real, something that will break through the barriers we've both built. But instead, she just nods. It's a small, almost imperceptible movement.

"Angelo, I need to know that you're not lying to me. I need to know that regardless of what shitstorm or fuckfest we encounter, I can depend on you to not screw me over. I also need to know that you're not going to treat me like a toy or piece of property. I know the men in the Cosa Nostra have a reputation for how they treat their women. I want this partnership to be different."

I'm silent for a moment. There are things she needs to know and this could be the time to tell her.

"I couldn't treat you like a toy or piece of property even if I wanted to. You're the heir to one of the largest syndicates in this country. You will have men bowing to you, falling to their knees to fulfill your every demand. God knows I might be one of them. You're the power, Sophia. I'm just here to help you see that. And yes, whatever happens we will face it as partners, equal partners. Together."

"Yeah," she says quietly. "Together."

"Sophia," I say. "The betrothal, it's not what you think it is. It's not really optional. If we don't get married, you will essentially forfeit your rights to the family name. I know it's antiquated and chauvinistic, but your father set things up this way to try and protect you."

"To protect me?" she says, her expression filled with distaste. "You keep saying that. I don't believe it."

"Listen to me, Sophia," I say to her, coming to sit beside her. I take her hand, willing her to understand.

"The ways of Cosa Nostra are practically set in stone. No female dons, no women in charge. Women who are cast off from powerful families or daughters without fathers are up for grabs. Your father wanted to be sure that you were protected from that, that you were allowed to take power without years of bloodshed."

"I don't want to marry you," she whispers, and I try to ignore the pain that her words cause me. I don't know why they should hurt. We only just met. It's reasonable that she wouldn't want to get married.

I lean forward and kiss her forehead. "I know, *Tesoro mio,*" I say back quietly. "We will pretend for now, but we need to be convincing. I will try to make sure that you don't have to do anything that you don't want to do. I promise you."

"I'm angry at you for keeping this from me," she says, her voice louder. She leans back to look at me, tears standing in her hazel eyes. They glimmer in the evening light, and I hate the small tremor in her lower lip.

"You should be," I tell her, my voice breaking a little on the words. I feel terrible, and I have to admit that Franco was right. I should have told her right away.

"I forgive you," she says, the tears slipping down her cheeks.

"You don't have to," I tell her.

"I have no choice," she argues, blinking and swiping at her tears. "None of you have left me any choice."

I can see the doubt in her eyes, the fear that maybe, just maybe, we won't make it through this. And for the first time, I'm not sure if I have the answers she needs.

But I will find them. For her, I will find them.

Even if it means risking my own safety in the process.

Chapter Nine

Sophia

The elevator doors slid open with a quiet chime, revealing the dimly lit, industrial-chic space that makes up Angelo's office. The decor is sparse but stylish—exposed brick walls, sleek furniture, and a large desk that dominates the room. Despite its minimalism, everything in here screams power.

I step inside, my heart pounding in my chest. This isn't just some run-of-the-mill introduction. This is part of rejoining the mafia world, my father's world, and now—whether I like it or not—it's mine. Angelo was right about one thing: I had to confront this head-on.

Angelo is already standing by the window, hands in his pockets, looking as composed as ever. His calm, collected demeanor is still irritating to me, especially when I feel like my nerves are about to snap. But my attention shifts when I see the man standing beside him.

He's tall, almost too lean, with a dark, brooding energy that makes the air feel a little heavier. His hair is slicked back and a shadow of stubble lines his jaw. He's dressed in black, from his tailored suit to the steel-toed boots that peek out from under his pant cuffs.

This is an old-school mafia man in new clothes. I remember men like him meeting with my father at all hours of the day and night. A true Sicilian mobster never fails to make my blood run cold.

"Franco," Angelo says smoothly, gesturing toward me, "this is Sophia Agostini."

Franco's eyes meet mine, and I feel the weight of his gaze—cold, assessing, like he's trying to read me with a single glance. He doesn't smile, doesn't even bother pretending to be polite.

He just stands there, arms crossed, like he isn't sure if he should shake my hand or toss me out the window. Honestly, I expect either thing in equal measure. I can't tell anything about his intentions when I look into his dark eyes.

For a stretch, he says nothing. His silence is almost unbearable.

I square my shoulders, refusing to be intimidated. "Nice to meet you, Franco," I say, my tone sharp.

"Is it?" he replies, his voice low and rough. He seems like he doesn't believe me for a second.

I raise an eyebrow. So, this is how it was going to be.

Angelo clears his throat, stepping forward to ease the tension. "Franco's my second-in-command. He'll be working with us while you're here, ensuring your safety."

"Good to know," I say, keeping my eyes on Franco, who hasn't moved an inch. He's standing so still, is so in control, that it almost makes me want to poke him just to see if he's human.

"Is that a problem for you?" Franco asks, his tone cool, almost bored.

I narrow my eyes, not appreciating his attitude. "Why would it be?"

"Because," he says, his gaze hardening, "you're the daughter of Carlo Agostini. That makes you more of a liability than an asset. For now."

I feel a spark of irritation flare in my chest. "I didn't ask for this," I shoot back. "I didn't ask to be part of this mess. But I'm here now, so the least you could do is pretend to trust me."

Franco's jaw clenches, but his expression doesn't change. "Trust is earned, not given."

I hold his gaze, refusing to back down. "I wasn't planning on asking for it."

Angelo, watching this exchange with an unreadable expression behind his glasses, finally steps in. "That's enough," he says firmly, cutting through the tension. "We're all on the same side here."

Franco says nothing, but I can see the flicker of annoyance in his eyes. He doesn't like me, that much is clear. But I'm not here to make friends—I'm here to survive. If he doesn't want to trust me, that's his problem.

Still, I can't help but feel a little slighted. Who the hell is Franco Pesci to judge me? He doesn't know what I've been through, what I've lost. I have spent my entire life running from the world he calls home, and now that I'm standing in the middle of it, I'm not going to let him treat me like I don't belong.

"I've been running from this my whole life," I say, my voice quieter, but no less steady. "But I'm not running anymore. Whether you like it or not, I'm part of this family."

Franco's eyes flicker over me, something unreadable passing behind them. He doesn't say anything, but I can tell I've struck a nerve.

Angelo glances between us, his brow furrowing slightly. "Franco, you know that she's here because she needs our help. She's under my protection."

Franco finally unfolds his arms, taking a step closer. His movements are slow, deliberate, like a predator sizing up its prey. "I don't care whose protection she's under," he says, his voice a low rumble. "As long as she doesn't get in the way."

I clench my fists, fighting the urge to snap back. But instead of responding with anger, I take a deep breath and meet his gaze head-on. "I don't plan to. But I'm not going to sit around and play the damsel, either."

For a moment, Franco doesn't react. He just looks at me, his dark eyes boring into mine, like he's searching for something. Then, slowly, a flicker of something—respect, maybe—crosses his features.

"Good," he finally says, his voice quieter but still rough around the edges. "Because this isn't a game, and you're not a spectator."

I nod, feeling the shift between us. Franco doesn't trust me, but he isn't dismissing me either. And for now, that's enough. Respect is a start. I can work on trust later.

Angelo, sensing the tension has diffused, claps Franco on the shoulder. "We've got a meeting soon. Sophia, you should head back to the penthouse. Franco and I will handle things for now."

"Right," I say, glancing at Angelo before turning back to Franco. "I'll let you get to it."

Angelo glances at his watch, clearly ready to wrap things up. "We should head to the meeting," he says, his tone all business again. But before I can react, he steps closer to me, his hand catching mine in a firm grip. The warmth of his touch sends a spark up my arm, catching me off guard.

He leans down, his mouth pressing a quick but hard kiss to mine, a show of possession that leaves my head spinning for a second. When he pulls back, his eyes linger on mine for a beat longer than necessary.

Franco raises an eyebrow, watching the exchange with a mixture of amusement and disbelief. "Well, that's one way to say goodbye," he mutters under his breath, arms still crossed as he eyed us both.

I shrug, trying to play it off, though my face probably gives me away. "We are betrothed after all."

Angelo shoots Franco a look, and I can see the flicker of warning in his eyes. "*Comportati*," he says in a low, commanding tone. I'm not fluent in Italian, but I'm pretty sure the word means something along the lines of "behave".

Franco gives a mock salute, the ghost of a smirk tugging at his lips. "*Capito*, boss," he replies dryly.

I have to stifle my giggle, biting my lip as I turn away, but Angelo catches the hint of my smile and squeezes my hand once more before letting go. "We'll be back soon," he says, his voice softer as his gaze meets mine again.

I'm not sure what to make of him yet, but one thing is clear: Franco Pesci is a force to be reckoned with.

And whether he likes it or not, I'm not going anywhere.

As I walk out of the office and head toward the elevator, I can't help but replay the conversation in my mind. Franco is tough, no doubt about that, but there is something else about him—something that makes me wonder if his hard exterior is just a front.

Angelo trusts him, that much is clear. And if Angelo trusts him, I'll have to find a way to make things work between us. I'm not looking for friends in this world, but if Franco is going to be part of my life now, we have to find some kind of common ground.

The elevator doors slide open, and I step inside, my mind already racing ahead to the next challenge.

Justine will be landing tomorrow, and I can't wait to see her, to have some piece of my old life back. Angelo was not pleased with the idea of bringing an innocent into this mess, but he had agreed to Justine flying out when I made it clear she would just do so on her own if she didn't hear from us soon.

As the elevator rises toward the penthouse, I can't shake the feeling that things are only going to get more complicated from here.

Franco is right about one thing—this isn't a game. And if I'm not careful, I could end up being just another casualty in a world that doesn't forgive mistakes.

Chapter Ten

Angelo

The streets of New York blur by as the car speeds through the city.

I sit in the backseat, my mind a battlefield of thoughts, every detail of the day replaying in my head. The feel of Sophia's hand in mine, the taste of her lips, and the weight of Franco's scrutinizing gaze all linger in my mind.

I have always prided myself on being in control—of my emotions, of my surroundings, of my life. But since Sophia showed up, everything has felt just a little more precarious.

Franco is silent beside me, his eyes fixed on the road ahead, but I know that won't last long. The man is like a hawk—always watching, always assessing. I can practically feel the questions brewing behind his cool, dark eyes.

Finally, after several blocks of tense silence, Franco shifts in his seat, turning to face me. "What are you doing with her, Angelo?" he asks, his voice low and steady, cutting straight to the point.

I don't look at him, keeping my gaze on the passing cityscape. "You know why she's here. We're protecting her."

"That's not what I'm asking, and you know it," he replies, his tone sharp. "If this is about keeping her safe, then fine. But if you're just fucking her because she's convenient or you think she's hot, then we've got a problem."

My jaw tightens, and I finally turn to meet his gaze. "And why's that?"

"Because there are plenty of hot women out there with a lot less baggage," Franco says bluntly. "You don't need to get mixed up with her if that's all this is. She's got enough shit to deal with. If you're not serious, walk away."

Anger flares in my chest, a cold, controlled burn that I barely keep from showing. "She's not just some woman, Franco. She's important to me."

Franco doesn't flinch, doesn't back down. "If she's important, then treat her like it. Because if you're not ready to deal with the fallout of all of this, you need to back off now."

I lean forward, my voice dropping to a dangerous whisper. "You're overstepping."

Franco's expression remains impassive, but I can see the tension in the set of his jaw. "Maybe. But someone's got to say it. You're not thinking straight when it comes to her, and that's dangerous—for both of you."

I glare at him, my fists clenching in my lap. "I know exactly what I'm doing."

He raises an eyebrow, his gaze piercing. "Do you? Because from where I'm standing, you're letting her get under your skin. And that's going to complicate things."

I hold his gaze, the car engine the only sound in the confined space. Franco is loyal, I know that, but he's also pragmatic—brutally so. He isn't afraid to speak the truth, no matter how much it stings.

"I'm handling it," I say finally, my voice cold as ice.

Franco studies me for a long moment, and then nods once, a subtle gesture of acquiescence. "Fine. But just know this—if you screw this up, it's not just your ass on the line. It's hers too."

Before I can respond, my phone buzzes in my pocket, interrupting the moment. I pull it out, glancing at the screen. The number is blocked, but I know exactly who it is.

"Costa," I mutter under my breath, the name tasting like poison on my tongue.

Franco's eyes darken, and he leans in slightly, listening as I answer the call.

"Angelo." A slick, oily voice oozes through the line, sending a shiver of disgust down my spine. "I hear you've been busy. Bringing dear Sophia back into the fold, hmm? How touching."

"Costa," I greet him, my voice flat, devoid of emotion. "I'd say it's nice to hear from you, but I'd be lying."

Giuseppe Costa chuckles, the sound smooth and pleasing. He has always been too slick by half, too inviting, too charming. His honeyed words and beautiful face have always been the perfect cover for his evil heart. "Come now, is that any way to greet family? After all, you've brought my sweet little niece home. I've missed her, you know."

I grit my teeth, fighting the urge to smash the phone against the dashboard. "She's not your niece, Costa. She's Carlo's daughter, and you're nothing to her."

"Oh, but you're wrong," Costa purrs, his voice dripping with condescension. "I'm all she has left of her dear papa's legacy. And I'd like to have a little family reunion, don't you think?"

I glance at Franco, who is watching me intently, his jaw clenched. He can hear every word, and I know he is already calculating the implications of this call.

"What do you want, Costa?" I ask, keeping my voice steady.

"What I've always wanted," Costa replies smoothly. "Control. Power. And right now, that little bird of yours is sitting on a very valuable perch. I want her, Angelo. Send her to me, and we can all walk away from this with our heads still attached."

"You know that's not going to happen," I say, my voice low and lethal. "She's betrothed to me. Her father left her as the family heir, and I will give her the license to claim it."

Costa sighs dramatically as if he's disappointed. "I had a feeling you'd say that. Which is why I've decided to give you a little incentive."

The line goes silent for a moment, and then I hear it—a scream, muffled and distant, but unmistakable. My blood runs cold.

"Who is that?" I demand, my voice sharp.

"Just a little friend of yours," Costa says, his tone sickeningly sweet. "Consider it a reminder that I'm not someone to be trifled with. You have until tomorrow to send her to me, Angelo. Or I start sending you pieces of what's left of your friend."

I feel a surge of rage, a white-hot fury that made my vision blur at the edges. "If you touch her, I swear..."

"Oh, I wouldn't dream of it," Costa interrupts, his voice dripping with false sincerity. "But accidents happen, you know? It would be such a shame if anything were to happen to someone you care about."

"I've never expected much from you, but even you should know what a mistake it would be to mess with me.

I'm sure tales of my possessiveness have spread far. You think touching anything of mine is a good idea?"

His laugh is dry and deep, the laugh of a wretched man with almost nothing to lose. In my line of work, I've discovered that everybody has something they want to protect by any means. Money, a loved one, something precious, the list goes on. Guiseppe has always lusted after power, and he will do anything to get it. It is the most precious thing to him.

Power comes from finding that thing your enemy would do anything to protect, and taking it from them, destroying it, or using it to your advantage. It's a skill I've had years to hone.

"Angelo, you talk too. much. I much preferred your father. He was a brutal son of a bitch, but he had actions. Bring Sophia to me and maybe I won't kill her. Last I saw her, she was beautiful and had tits that would make a dead man hard. I'm sure I could find a use for her here."

Regardless of how vile this man is, I can't show him how much I care for Sophia. That would only be putting a target on her back. I have to play this smart. Guiseppe is smart enough to know how power works too.

"That's sick, even for you. But, I guess I shouldn't expect more from someone who couldn't even wait for his brother's corpse to get cold before trying to take his throne. You're such trash. I wouldn't even let your blood stain my shoes after I killed you."

The call ends abruptly, the line going dead in my hand. I stare at the phone, my heart pounding, a thousand scenarios racing through my mind.

Franco's voice cuts through the haze of anger. "What did he say?"

"He's got someone," I reply, my voice tight. "I don't know who, but he's using them as leverage."

Franco swears under his breath, his eyes flashing with anger. "We need to find out who and where he's keeping them. Fast."

I nod, already formulating a plan. "Get the team on it. I want every possible lead tracked down. No stone should be left unturned."

Franco doesn't hesitate, pulling out his own phone and barking orders to the team. The calm, controlled demeanor he usually displays is gone, replaced by the same cold fury that is burning through me.

As the car pulls up to our destination, I feel the full weight of what is happening settling over me. Costa has made his move, and it's only a matter of time before we are dragged into a full-blown war.

But I'm not going to let him win. Not this time. Not ever.

As we step out of the car, Franco turns to me, his expression grim. "We're in this now, Angelo. All of us. No turning back."

I nod, cold determination settling into my bones. "I know."

And with that, we walk into the building, ready to face whatever comes next. Because this is no longer just a fight for survival, it's a fight for everything—and I'm not about to lose.

I storm into the building, the adrenaline coursing through my veins like a shot of pure fire. My mind is a battlefield of rage and cold calculation, every thought focused on one thing: making Costa pay.

Franco is on the phone, coordinating with the team to track down every possible lead on Costa's location. I can see the tension in his posture, the same tightness that is coiled in my gut. We don't have time to waste. Every second is another moment Costa has to do more damage.

My phone buzzes in my pocket, and I pull it out, expecting the worst. But it's a message from one of our informants, a rat we'd planted in Costa's operations months ago.

Heard something. The young kid, your guy. He's in one of Costa's safe houses near the docks. Not good, boss. Not good at all.

I stare at the message, my grip tightening on the phone until my knuckles turn white. "It's one of our own," I mutter to Franco, the anger in my voice barely contained. "The kid I've been training, Luca. He's only nineteen. They've got him near the docks."

Franco's eyes darken, a flicker of something dangerous crossing his face. "Shit. Costa's going for blood."

I nod, my mind already spinning through options. "We need to move fast. Get the team ready—we're going to bring him home."

Franco is already making the call, but I grab his arm before he can head out. "Go to the penthouse first," I order, my voice steely. "Stay with Sophia. I don't want Costa making a move on her while we're out. She's priority number one."

Franco looks like he wants to argue, his brow furrowing, but he knows better. He nods sharply, his expression hard. "Understood. I'll have men on standby to back you up at the docks."

I clap him on the shoulder, silent agreement passing between us. "Keep her safe, Franco."

"I will," he promises, his voice resolute. With that, he turns and heads out, his footsteps echoing in the hallway as he leaves to fulfill his duty. I don't have to worry about Sophia—not with Franco watching over her.

Now, I can focus on what needs to be done.

The docks are deserted, the cold air biting at my skin as we move in silence, the team flanking me on all sides. The informant's tip had been good—we'd traced Costa's men to a run-down warehouse, the kind of place you could burn to the ground without anyone asking questions.

As we approach, I can see the faint glow of light seeping through the cracks in the walls, and I can hear the sound of muffled voices filtering through the night. My blood boils with each step closer, every fiber of my being screaming for revenge.

The kid—Luca—has been with us for barely a year. He's young, green, but he has potential. I see something in him, something that reminds me of myself at his age. And now, because of Costa, that potential might be snuffed out before it has a chance to flourish.

I signal to the men, and we move in, silently breaching the perimeter of the warehouse. The doors creak as we push them open, revealing a scene that makes my stomach turn.

Luca is tied to a chair in the center of the room, his face a mess of blood and bruises. He's slumped over, unconscious—or worse. But it's his hands that catch my attention. Blood-soaked rags are wrapped around them, but even from where I stand, I can see the damage. Two of his fingers have been cut off, the stumps crudely bandaged in a way that makes it clear Costa's men wanted to keep him alive, but in pain.

"Bastards," I hiss under my breath, my vision going red with rage.

One of Costa's goons turns at the sound, eyes widening in shock as he sees us. He reaches for his gun, but I'm faster.

I fire a single shot, and he crumples to the ground, dead before he even hits the floor.

The rest of the team moves in quickly, taking down the remaining guards with brutal efficiency. Within minutes, the warehouse is silent, except for the labored breathing of my men and the faint whimpering from Luca.

I rush to his side, kneeling beside him. His eyes flutter open, glazed with pain and fear, but there is a spark of recognition when he sees me.

"Boss..." he croaks, his voice barely a whisper.

"Don't talk," I order, my tone softer than before. I reach for the ropes binding his hands, cutting them loose with a swift motion. "We're getting you out of here."

Luca's head lolls to the side, his body limp from exhaustion and blood loss. He's in bad shape, but he's alive. That's all that mattered. "I'm sorry..." he mumbles, his voice cracking. "I tried to..."

"You did good," I interrupt, my voice firm. "You held on. That's all I ask of any of your guys."

I turn to one of the men. "Get him to the car. Take him to Doc—tell him to do whatever it takes."

The man nods, gently lifting Luca in his arms as he carries him out of the warehouse. I watch them go, my heart heavy with the knowledge of what has been done to Luca. But there's no time for guilt—only for action.

I stand, the fire in my veins rekindling as I turn my attention back to the warehouse. Costa thought he could get away with this. He thought he could hurt one of mine and walk away unscathed.

He's wrong.

"Search the place," I order, my voice cold as steel. "I want to know if Costa left anything behind."

The men fan out, combing the warehouse for anything of value. It doesn't take long before one of them calls out, "Boss, over here."

I walk over to find them standing by a large set of crates, the wood splintered and worn. I recognized the markings immediately—Costa's usual method of smuggling contraband into the country. He has connections at the ports, enough to get questionable shipments through customs without so much as a raised eyebrow.

"These are his," I say, my voice dark with satisfaction. "Open them."

The men pry the crates open, revealing their contents. My eyes narrow as I take in what's inside. High-end electronics, pharmaceuticals, and—most damning of all—illegal weapons. Guns, ammo, and explosives, all of which were strictly black market. Costa has been preparing for a war, and he has been stupid enough to leave his stockpile unguarded.

I run my fingers over one of the guns, the metal cold and deadly under my touch. Costa has smuggled this shipment in through his usual channels, greasing the palms of customs officials and port workers to ensure it could pass through without a hitch. But now it's in my hands, and I know exactly what to do with it.

"Millions of dollars, easy," one of my men mutters, shaking his head as he surveys the contents of the crates.

"And now it's worthless," I reply, a cold smile curling my lips. "Set it on fire. I want Costa to know exactly what happens when he crosses me."

The men don't hesitate, dousing the crates with gasoline we find stored in the warehouse. The acrid smell fills the air as the liquid soaks into the wood, pooling around the base of the crates.

I stand back, watching as one of the men strikes a match and tosses it onto the gasoline-soaked wood. The flames roar to life, climbing higher and higher as they consume the crates. The fire spreads quickly, licking at the walls and ceiling, turning everything in its path to ash.

Costa's shipment—his entire investment—is going up in smoke. And with it, any leverage he thinks he has over me.

I watch the flames dance, the heat searing against my skin, but it's not enough to quench the fire burning inside me. Costa has hurt one of my own, and this is just the beginning. He will keep doing things like this until he gets his way, or we kill him.

Costa has taken something from me. Now, I'm going to take everything from him.

The fire roars behind us as we drive away, the smoke billowing into the night sky like a beacon. I know it wouldn't be long before Costa gets word of what I've done. And when he does, the message will be clear: I'm not someone to be fucked with.

As we make our way back to the city, I pull out my phone and dial Franco's number. He answers on the first ring.

"Everything secure at the penthouse?" I ask, my voice steady, though my heart is still racing.

"Secure," Franco confirms. "Sophia's safe. She doesn't know anything about what happened yet."

"Good," I reply, feeling a small measure of relief. "I'm on my way back. We need to discuss our next move."

There's a pause on the other end, and then Franco speaks again, his tone quieter. "You did the right thing, Angelo, but Costa won't forget this."

"I don't want him to," I say, my voice hardening. "I want him to suffer."

And with that, I end the call, leaning back in the seat as I stare out the window. The city lights blur past, a stark contrast to the darkness that still simmers in my chest.

This isn't over—not by a long shot. Costa has made his move, and I've answered. But I know, deep down, that this is only the beginning.

And I'm ready for whatever comes next.

Chapter Eleven

Sophia

The morning sun filters through the floor-to-ceiling windows of the penthouse, casting long shadows across the polished marble floors.

I've been up for hours, pacing the living room as I try to keep my mind from spiraling. Coming back to New York has dredged up so many memories—some sweet, most of them bitter—and the weight of it all is starting to feel like too much.

A knock at the door snaps me out of my thoughts. I walk over and open it to find Angelo's right-hand man, Franco Pesci, standing there. He has the kind of intense, watchful presence that tells you he's always assessing, always on guard. It makes me nervous when he turns that sharp gaze on me, but strangely, I also feel safer now that he is here.

"Franco," I greet him, trying to keep my voice steady. "Is everything okay?"

He nods, his face blank. "Angelo asked me to check in with you. He had to take care of some business, but he'll be back shortly."

"Of course he did," I mutter under my breath, not entirely surprised. Angelo is nothing if not thorough, and having me watched is probably just another one of the things that he thinks of as his duty. "Well, as you can see, I'm still here, safe and sound."

Franco doesn't smile, but there's a slight softening around his eyes. "Good to hear. But we need to discuss something important."

I raise an eyebrow, crossing my arms over my chest. "Go on."

"Giuseppe Costa," he says, his tone turning cold at the mention of the name. "He's been making moves. His men are in the city, and it's clear they're looking for you."

The name sends a chill down my spine. Costa. He was my father's right-hand man for years, a ruthless, calculating bastard who always made my skin crawl as a child. When my father died, Costa had clearly seen it as his opportunity to seize power. With me back in the picture, I was now the biggest threat to his ambitions.

"Why come after me?" I ask, even though I already know the answer. "Why not just take over the Agostini family and be done with it?"

"Because he needs legitimacy," Franco replies, his voice hard. "Without you, there's no one to officially pass the mantle to. He can't take control without making sure he has a rightful claim to put forth. And the easiest way to do that is by getting rid of you."

I swallow hard, the gravity of the situation sinking in. I knew coming back to New York would be dangerous, but hearing the truth laid out so plainly makes it all the more real. Costa isn't just a threat—he's a predator, and I'm his prey.

"Great," I say, my voice sharp with sarcasm. "So I'm just supposed to hide out here while you and Angelo play bodyguard?"

Franco's eyes narrow slightly, and for a moment, I think I see a flicker of something in them—respect, maybe? "You're here because it's the safest place for you to be. But that doesn't mean you're helpless. We need to figure out our next move, and we need to do it fast."

I nod, feeling the weight of the decision pressing down on me. "Right. Well, I'll do whatever it takes. But I'm not going to be a pawn in this, Franco. If Costa wants to come after me, I'm not just going to sit here and wait for him to make his move."

He studies me for a moment, his gaze piercing. "I respect that. But you need to trust us. Angelo's put everything in place to protect you. We're not taking any chances."

I hold his gaze, matching his intensity with my own. "I appreciate that, but I'm not just some damsel in distress. I need to know what's happening, and I need to be part of the plan."

There's a long pause, and then, to my surprise, Franco gives a curt nod. "Fair enough. We'll keep you in the loop. But understand this—if it comes down to it, your safety is the priority. No heroics, no risks."

"Deal," I say, feeling a strange sense of relief. It isn't much, but it was a start. At least now, I know where I stand with Franco.

"Good," he says, and just like that, the conversation is over. "Angelo will be back soon. I'll let you know when he arrives."

I watch as he turns to leave, his movements precise, almost mechanical. But just before he reaches the door, he hesitates, turning back to face me.

"You've been through a lot," he says quietly. "But you're stronger than most people would be in your situation. Your father would be proud of you. Just remember that."

I blink, caught off guard by the unexpected compliment. "Thanks, Franco. That…means a lot."

He nods once, then leaves without another word, the door clicking shut behind him. I let out a breath I didn't realize I was holding, my mind spinning with everything he's just told me.

Costa is here, in the city, and he is hunting me. But I'm not going to let him win. I can't, there is too much at stake.

I'm about to head back to the windows when my phone chimes, snapping me out of my thoughts. It's a text from Justine, and a wave of relief washed over me. I need a distraction, something to keep me from spiraling any further.

Just landed. Can't wait to see you, babe! Also, do I get a hot mafia bodyguard? ;)

I can't help but smile at the message. Justine has a way of making everything feel a little less dire, even when the world is crumbling around me.

I quickly reply.

Can't wait to see you too. The car is on its way to pick you up. And as for the bodyguard… we'll see. ;)

With that, I grab my coat and go to find Franco. I want to get Justine from the airport, to fill her in on everything, and to remind myself that I'm not in this alone. And knowing Justine, she'll probably have some choice words for the whole situation—along with a few jokes to lighten the mood.

Chapter Twelve

Sophia

The black SUV pulls up to the curb outside the airport, the hum of the engine filling the silence as I wait for Justine to appear.

I drum my fingers against the armrest, my nerves still frayed from the conversation with Franco and the weight of everything that has happened since I arrived in New York. But the thought of seeing Justine, of having a piece of my old life back, delivers a flicker of warmth to the cold knot in my chest.

And then I see her—tall, blonde, and impossibly glamorous, even after a transatlantic flight. Justine is the kind of woman who turns heads without trying, her presence commanding attention the moment she steps into view. She spots me through the car window and breaks into a grin, waving enthusiastically as she approaches.

"Sarah!" she calls out, using my old name. It makes my heart pang, but I don't correct her. Not yet. Not when she's about to be thrown into the middle of everything.

I push open the door and step out to meet her. "Sophia," I remind her with a smile, pulling her into a tight hug. The familiar scent of her perfume, the feel of her arms around me—it's like a balm for my frayed nerves.

"Right, right. Sophia Agostini, Mafia Princess," she teases, her eyes twinkling with mischief as she pulls back to look at me. "God, it's good to see you."

"It's good to see you too," I reply, my voice softer than I intended. "I've missed you."

"Missed you too, love," she says, looping her arm through mine as we turn back toward the car. "Now, let's get out of here. I need a shower, a drink, and a full update on whatever the hell is going on in your life."

"You and me both," I mutter, leading her to the car.

Just as we get close, the door opens, and Franco climbs out. His hawk-like eyes survey the area around us before he places one of his hands on each of our shoulders, and hustles us into the car. Justine makes a very British sound of protest at being handled in such a manner, but I follow Franco without question.

"No loitering about in the open," he says firmly, sliding in beside me and slamming the door. "Drive," he says to the man in the driver's seat.

If steam could come out of someone's ears, Justine would be ready to boil over. I see her open her mouth to say something particularly direct and cutting, but then Franco turns to look at her. There's a moment of silence as they stare at one another, and Justine blinks as if she's surfacing from underwater.

"Hot Italian bodyguard, I see," she says, recovering neatly.

I giggle. "Something like that," I admit, glancing at Franco. "He wasn't wrong. We shouldn't have been wandering around in plain sight like that."

"Thank you for rescuing me from certain danger," Justine says, her English accent soft inviting, delightfully foreign. She bats her eyes a little at Franco, and I roll mine. I've seen this song and dance before. It usually works for my friend, but Franco is a totally different kind of man than the guys that Justine is used to flirting with.

"Don't mention it," Franco says, his tone civil, and dare I say it...inviting. I glance at him in annoyance. I've spent the entire time I've been here trying to get into his good graces and Justine seems to have won him over within seconds of her arrival.

"Tell me," Justine says to him coyly, "do you have time to guard me as well as Sar...Sophia?"

I sigh, shaking my head, but I smile anyway. I can't help but feel a strange sense of relief. Justine was still Justine, even in the face of danger and uncertainty, and that made everything a little more bearable.

The ride back to the penthouse is filled with chatter, Justine's excitement bubbling over as she peppers me with questions about New York, the penthouse, and—of course—Angelo. I answer as best as I can, skirting around the more dangerous details. I know it won't be long before she starts digging deeper.

When we arrive at the penthouse, Justine steps out first, her eyes widening as she takes in the grandeur of the building. "Blimey," she breathes, spinning in a slow circle to take it all in. "You weren't kidding when you said this place was posh."

"It's something," I agree, motioning for her to follow me inside. "Come on, I'll show you around."

"Coming with us, Franco?" Justine asks over her shoulder as we walk into the lobby of the building.

He nods, his expression as stoic as ever, but I catch the subtle way his eyes flicker over to Justine, narrowing slightly in assessment. "Just doing my job," he replies, his tone clipped.

Justine nods at him. "Just so," she says to him primly. She snakes her arm through mine. "Is it in the water, or the food they eat here? Do they all look like this?" she whispers *sotto voce* at me.

I have to bite back a laugh, knowing full well that Franco's guarded exterior is about to get a serious test.

"This is Franco Pesci," I finally introduce him. "He's Angelo's second-in-command."

"Franco," Justine repeats, her voice practically purring as she steps closer, her hand extended. "Pleasure to officially meet you."

Franco hesitates for the briefest moment before taking her hand, his grip firm but careful, as if he isn't quite sure what to do. "Likewise," he says, his voice lower than usual. But I notice the slight twitch at the corner of his mouth. It's the first crack I have ever seen in his otherwise impenetrable demeanor.

He tries to take back his hand, but Justine holds on tighter. I'm no expert in made men, but I know for a fact that if someone was as built and as fucking intimidating as Franco, if they wanted to fling a whole human across the room, it would be a walk in Central Park for him to do so.

Yet, here he was, trapped by the dainty fingers of my best friend and her fluttering lashes. Not that I could blame him of course. I'd seen lesser men fall before Justine's siren eyes and her sharp as-needles tongue.

He looked so out of his element, standing there with his hand in hers. I thought the tips of his ears might even be turning red.

Justine's smile widened. "So, Franco, what exactly does a second-in-command do around here? Besides looking, hot as fuck and good enough to eat, of course."

I watch with amusement as Franco's jaw tightens, but there's something else in his eyes—something that had flickered to life the moment she touched him. I knew Franco well enough by now to recognize when he was affected by someone, and Justine, with her boldness and charm, had clearly thrown him off balance.

"My job is to make sure everything runs smoothly," Franco replies, his tone carefully controlled, though I can hear the hint of tension beneath it. "And that includes keeping an eye on anyone who might be a threat."

"Oh, a threat?" Justine echoes, her eyes gleaming with mischief. "Are you saying I'm dangerous? Will you have to pin me down and make me confess all the bad, bad things I have done? I should let you know that I prefer traditional ropes to handcuffs."

"Okay, ease up, tiger. You're going to give the man a stroke, and then I'll have to revive him."

"What? I haven't done anything. I'm simply asking the man if I'm a looming danger." She turns back to him, her winning smile slipping right back into place.

Franco's gaze locks onto hers, and for a moment, it feels like the air around us has shifted. "That remains to be seen," he finally says, his voice dropping.

I have to stifle a laugh, watching the sparks fly between them. Justine, ever the flirt, is clearly enjoying the effect she's having on Franco. And Franco, for all his coldness, isn't immune to her charms.

"All right, you two," I interject, deciding it's best to intervene before things get out of hand. "Let's not get carried away. Justine, I'll take you to the apartment I've set up for you, and Franco…I'm sure you've got important 'second-in-command' things to do?"

Franco's eyes flick over to me, a flash of something in his gaze before he gives a curt nod. "Of course. I'll leave you to it."

Justine pouts playfully, but she lets go of his hand, though not before giving him one last lingering look. "I'm sure we'll see each other again soon, Franco," she says with a wink.

Franco's expression doesn't change, but I can see the way his eyes follow her as we walk away, his usual stoicism faltering just a little. Justine got under his skin, and I have a feeling this is only the beginning of whatever is brewing between them.

As we get into the elevator to go to the apartment I'd arranged for Justine, I can't help but smile to myself. Franco is curious about my friend, that much is clear, but whether that's a good thing or not remains to be seen.

***

The apartment I had set up for Justine is just a few floors down from the penthouse. It wasn't as grand as Angelo's floor, but it's safe, secure, and most importantly, private.

"This is fantastic, Sophia," Justine says as we step inside, her eyes lighting up as she takes in the space. "You really didn't have to go all out like this."

"I wanted to," I reply, watching as she explores the living room. "You deserve a nice place to stay. And I wanted you to be close, just in case..."

Justine turned to me, her expression softening. "In case what?"

"In case things get...complicated," I admit, my voice trailing off. "This isn't just a holiday, Justine. There's a lot going on and I don't want you caught in the crossfire."

She walks over to me, placing a hand on my arm. "Hey, I'm here because you're my best friend. And we agreed that you wouldn't patronize me by diluting the facts, right?"

"J..."

"Right, Sarah?" she pins me with a look that is clearly meant to pull at my heartstrings.

"Right. I'm sorry. I don't know the full details yet, but there's a power struggle going on. My father's position needs to be filled. I'm the one, his only heir, and naturally, the mantle falls to me. But there's someone else who wants it and he's trying to kill me. As long as I'm alive, he will never have a legitimate claim to power."

She's uncharacteristically quiet for a few minutes before she speaks.

"I'd say that's all poppycock, but I know you're not one to dick around. Damn, when did our lives slip into a bad remake of *The Godfather*?"

My chuckle is light, but it's nice to feel like laughing about my situation.

"I think the thing I'm most scared of is finding out that my mother lied to me my whole life. She told me that my dad was this monstrous person that she had to get me away from, but coming here and learning more about him...it doesn't seem that way. Also, he apparently knew where we were all those years, yet he never came looking. That must mean something, right?"

"Right. If he was truly a heartless monster, he would've come to drag you both back home."

"Exactly." I exhale and plop down on the sofa.

"She was going to tell me something, that day in the hospital. The day she..." I swallow, unable to get the words out. Justine reaches out to squeeze my hand.

"She was going to say something, but she never got to say it. What if she lied to me about this? What do I do then?"

"Honey, I think you have to remember that she was not much older than you are now when she took you and ran. She must've been scared out of her mind and alone. If she went through all of that, she must've had good reason. Your mother loved you and never would've done anything to intentionally hurt you. You know that, right?"

I nod, and she takes my hand in hers.

"Whatever's going on, we'll deal with it together. Got it?"

I nodded, grateful for her unwavering support. "Got it."

She gives me a reassuring smile, then glances around the room again. "Now, if you don't mind, I'm going to take a long, hot bath, during which I may or may not be thinking about a certain made man."

"Oh, my goodness Justine."

She rolls her eyes and goes right on talking.

"And then I'll settle in. Maybe have a drink or three."

I laughed, feeling some of the tension ease. "Sounds like a plan. I'll leave you to it."

Justine pulls me into another quick hug before heading to the bedroom. I watch her go, a small part of me wishing I could stay here with her, away from the chaos that awaits me back at the penthouse.

But I can't. I have to go back, and I have to face whatever is waiting for me there.

***

When I return to the penthouse, the atmosphere has shifted, the air thick with tension. I barely have time to process the change, before Angelo appears in the doorway, his eyes wild. My stomach does a flip.

"Where on earth have you been?" he demands, his voice low and dangerous.

I blink, taken aback by the intensity in his tone. "I was taking Justine to her place. What's…"

"Everyone, out," Angelo barks, his voice cutting through the air like a whip. The few men who are in the room scatter.

I don't have time to react before Angelo crosses the room in a few quick strides, grabbing me by the arms and pulling me close. His lips crash down on mine with a ferocity that leaves me breathless, his grip bruising as he kisses me hard.

I gasp against his mouth, my mind reeling from the sudden onslaught of emotions—anger, fear, desire, all tangled together in a chaotic mess. I try to push him away, but his hold on me is unyielding, his body pressing against mine, demanding.

When he finally pulls back, we are both breathing hard, our foreheads pressed together as he holds me close, his hands still gripping my arms.

"Don't you ever do that again," he growls, his voice rough with anger. "Do you have any idea what could have happened to you?"

I stare up at him, my heart pounding in my chest. "I'm not your prisoner, Angelo. I can take care of myself."

"Not when Costa is out there, waiting for an opportunity to strike," he snaps, his eyes blazing with fury. "You don't get it, Sophia. You're not safe out there. Not without me."

I glare back at him, refusing to back down. "I'm not some damsel in distress, Angelo. I'm not going to sit around and let you control my every move."

"You don't have a choice," he shoots back, his grip tightening. "You're in my world now, and in my world, there are rules. Rules that keep you alive."

"Is that what this is about?" I demand, my voice rising. "Keeping me alive so you can control me?"

"No," he says, his voice dropping to a dangerous whisper. "It's about keeping you alive because I can't lose you."

The words hang between us, heavy and raw, and for a moment, the anger between us shifts into something else—something darker, more primal.

His eyes lock onto mine, and I see the storm of emotions swirling there—fear, desire, possessiveness. I know what is coming before it even happens, and I brace myself for the impact.

With a low growl, Angelo's lips find mine again, his hands roaming over my body with a desperation that matches the fire burning inside me. I can't think, can't breathe—there's only him, his touch, his taste, the way he consumes me completely.

He backs me up against the wall, his mouth never leaving mine as he tears at my clothes, his hands rough and demanding, groping and squeezing. I meet his intensity with my own, my fingers clawing at his shirt, desperate to feel his skin against mine.

He lifts me against the wall, and I hike my legs higher around his waist, my already short dress hiking higher up my body.

"You fucking torture me *Tesoro mio.*" He strokes a path up my inner thigh, igniting flames on my skin, and when he presses two fingers against my hot center, I move against him, grinding my pelvis against his, feeling his hardness.

"I can't think straight with you near. I should leave you like this now, dripping. Maybe then you'll understand a small bit of the frustration I feel."

He tries to withdraw his fingers, but I grab hold of his hand.

"Stop now, and I'll kill you before Guiseppe gets the chance."

"My ferocious beauty, you will make an astounding leader."

Hearing that from him, especially when I've been doubting myself all week, does something inexplicable to me. I guide his fingers back to where I crave them the most, and he deftly shifts my underwear aside and uncsremoniously thrusts two fingers inside of me.

"Fuck, yes." My voice is a husky rasp as I move against his fingers hungrily, desperate for him, wanting to be filled with him.

"You're always so ready for me. So deliciously tight."

He pulls down the sleeves of my dress, taking my flimsy lace bra with it. The chill puckers my nipples, turning them to hard beads, which Angelo rolls between his thumb and forefinger. I barely have time to realize what is about to happen before I come with a staggering intensity.

I feel a spatter of moisture drench my thighs as I writhe against him, gasping, clawing for purchase, nearly dizzy with pleasure.

He doesn't give me a break as his mouth latches onto my breast, sucking, biting, squeezing, and molding.

"More, please," I manage to say when coherent thought returns.

I find his belt buckle, undoing it and opening his fly, smiling when his cock springs free in my palm, heavy and hot. He makes a low sound in his throat as I fist it and pull a little.

"I should be scared of this thing," I say and press a kiss to his neck and down his exposed neck. "It destroys me, but heaven help me, I can't stop wanting to be torn apart." And then I guide him into me.

"Angelo," I gasp as he fills me, stretching me painfully. His name is a plea on my lips as he lifts me, wrapping my legs around his waist more tightly.

He makes a guttural sound that sends shivers down my spine, his hands gripping my hips as he drives into me with a force that takes my breath away.

We move together in a frenzy of need and frustration, every thrust a wordless declaration of the emotions we can't put into words.

"Oh God, Angelo!" I cry as the pleasure coils tighter and tighter within me. I held on to his shoulders for dear life as his thrusts increased in pace and velocity. My second orgasm crashes into me, making my legs shake and quiver.

"By God, you're beautiful," he grinds out, and then I feel the heat of his release inside of me. He presses his forehead against my shoulder as he comes apart, managing to support us even as he twitches and jerks with pleasure.

"Fuck," I murmur as my pussy clenches a few more times around his thickness. "Holy fuck."

For a moment, there's only silence, the room filled with the aftermath of our passion. Then Angelo's grip on me loosens. He allows me to slip down his body, and I feel a momentary pang of sorrow when his dick slides out of me. His hands slide to cradle my face as he presses his forehead against mine.

"Sophia..." He caresses my cheek, running his hand down my face tracing the angry red marks of a sharp, biting kiss that he placed on my neck.

"I hurt you." His voice is whisper soft and so pained that it tugs at my heartstrings.

"No, you didn't. If I had wanted you to stop, I would've asked you to, and you would have."

It surprises me how strongly I believe that. Angelo would never hurt me.

"If I wasn't deeply exhausted, I would be begging you to do it again."

I press my mouth softly against his, and his tongue darts out to stroke my lips.

"I'll be gentler next time," he says.

"Only if I want you to be," I retort, and he chuckles.

"Don't ever scare me like that again," he whispers, his voice raw with emotion.

I nod, too spent to argue, my heart still racing as I try to catch my breath. "I'm sorry," I whisper back, the words slipping out before I can stop them. "I didn't mean to worry you."

I don't know what's happening, but we are moving into uncharted territory. This is clearly a business arrangement made to benefit us, but the lines are beginning to blur uncomfortably.

He kisses me again, softer this time, his touch more tender as he pulls me close. "I just need you safe, Sophia.

This isn't going to work if I'm worrying about your safety every minute of the day."

That makes me roll my eyes, and I step away from him.

"Tell me what happened," I say finally, pulling back just enough to meet his eyes. "With Costa."

Angelo's expression darkens, the tension returning as he recounts the events of the day—the discovery of Luca, the condition they found him in, and the retaliation that followed. As he speaks, I see the cold, ruthless side of him that I have only glimpsed before. This is the part of him that will stop at nothing to protect what is his.

And as much as it scares me, I can't deny that part of me that is drawn to it, to him. It's never fun to discover that you might be deeply psychologically damaged. Being this strongly attracted to the darkness in another human must mean something negative about me. I briefly wonder if the problem is in my DNA. Maybe this was always inevitable.

When he finishes, I nod, processing everything he has said. "He won't stop," I say quietly, more to myself than to him. "Costa won't stop until he gets what he wants."

"Neither will I," Angelo replies, his voice hard as steel. "But I promise you this—he'll regret ever coming after us."

It only makes sense at this point to give Costa what he wants and I said as much to Angelo. He narrows his eyes.

"We can't, *Tesoro mio*. If we give in even once, everyone will suspect that we are weak. We will never stop fighting them off. Costa will just be the first of many people who want to topple you off your throne."

I sigh, pinching the bridge of my nose with two fingers. "A throne I don't even want," I mutter. I pace around the room, thinking.

"He wants us to show up to fight him. We'll do that. He expects a dainty little princess who doesn't know anything about defending herself, but I haven't lived the last twenty years of my life like a fugitive without learning how not just to survive, but to thrive." I stop and turn to face Angelo.

"If it's a war he wants, let's give him one. If my people are asking where their leader is, let's show them. I'm done hiding, Angelo. I'm done letting other people call the shots for me."

He watches me for a minute without saying anything, and then he steps forward, touching me in a way that feels like he isn't even aware that he is touching me.

"Good. They won't see the hell coming."

I believe him. And for the first time since all of this started, I feel a flicker of hope. We are in this together, and whatever happens next, we will face it side by side.

Because in this world, he's as much a weapon as any gun. And I have every intention of wielding him to the fullest.

Chapter Thirteen

Angelo

The room buzzes with tension, thick and palpable. I stand at the head of the table, Sophia next to me, her posture straight and composed. It's the same table her father had ruled from—where decisions were made, lives were changed and power was consolidated. But today, it isn't Carlo Agostini holding the reins.

It's his daughter.

I scan the faces of the men seated before us. These are the remnants of Carlo's old guard, men who have served him loyally for years, and a few others who have risen in rank since his death.

Their expressions range from skeptical to outright hostile, especially Giuseppe Costa. Carlo's former right-hand man has had his glare locked on Sophia the entire time, as though he can't believe she has had the audacity to stand before him.

Costa has been working to turn the loyalty of the others into a weapon, spreading rumors and stoking their doubts. He thinks he can fracture the family, claim leadership by undermining Sophia before she can even take her place. Sophia stands tall, despite the weight of their scrutiny.

Her composure is admirable, but I can feel the tension in her stance. This isn't just about taking on her father's legacy. It's about surviving in a world where people like Costa would rather see her dead than in charge.

I clear my throat, pulling everyone's attention back to me. "Gentlemen, thank you for coming. As many of you know, Carlo Agostini's death left a gap in this family—a gap that needs to be filled."

A murmur ripples through the room. I let it simmer for a moment before continuing. "That's why I've called you here today. Sophia Agostini, his only heir, will be stepping into the role of don to lead this family."

The murmuring stops. Silence falls heavily and all eyes turn to Sophia. Her chin lifts a little higher, her hazel-green eyes scanning the room as though daring anyone to challenge her. I can feel the tension rolling off her, but to her credit, she doesn't flinch. She's stronger than most would give her credit for.

Predictably, it's Guiseppe who speaks first. He leans back in his chair, his arms crossed over his chest. "A woman can't lead this family. You know that as well as I do, Castiglia. This isn't the local PTA. This is the Cosa Nostra."

The statement hangs in the air like a slap, and then I see the flicker of anger cross Sophia's face. I had expected Guiseppe to make trouble—he'd been a thorn in our side since Carlo's death in every way, quietly gathering his own supporters. He sees himself as the rightful successor, despite having no real claim to the family.

"I don't take orders from women," Guiseppe adds, his voice dripping with disdain. "Besides, this family needs a leader who understands how to handle power, not someone who's spent her life running from it."

The room is silent and all eyes shift to Sophia. I see the anger flash in her eyes, but she keeps her composure, her chin lifting a fraction as she faces the room. I note the flaring of her nostrils that indicates that she's breathing hard, but she looks steely, composed and dangerous. I feel a frisson of lust shiver over my skin.

"I may not have been raised in this life," she says, her voice clear and strong, "but I was born into it. And I have every intention of protecting the family my father built. That's more than I can say for those who've been trying to tear it apart from within."

Her gaze lands on Guiseppe, and the tension in the room thickens.

"You think you deserve to lead because you're the son of someone important?" she asks, her tone sharp. "Or because you've been spreading whispers and turning the men against me behind closed doors?"

A few of the men shift uncomfortably in their seats, exchanging uneasy glances. The truth of what Sophia has said is undeniable—Costa has been sowing discord for weeks, hoping to tip the balance in his favor. He has his followers, but not enough to make a direct move. Not yet.

Guiseppe's smirk faltered slightly, but he didn't back down. He's still a handsome man, although dissipation is starting to show around the edges. He reminds me of a rose that is just starting to fade from full glory, the brown of rot slowly curling the tips of the petals.

"A woman can't lead this family," he asserts. "You don't have the experience. You don't have the strength. You've been gone for years and you come back expecting us to bow to you because of your last name?"

I can feel Sophia's muscles tense beside me, but before I can step in, she takes another step forward.

"Strength?" she echoes, her voice dangerously soft. "You think that's what you have, Guiseppe? You think spreading lies and playing politics behind people's backs makes you a strong leader?" She snorts and leans forward on the table. She yanks back the sleeve of the suit she wore to this meeting, pressing the delicate skin of her wrist forward.

"The Cosa Nostra might not respect women, but it respects one thing above all else: blood." She nods sharply down at her exposed wrist, the blue veins standing out starkly as she stretches her wrist forward. "The blood flowing through my veins is the blood of royalty. I was born for this, forged for it even, and the blood flowing through my veins is a far greater claim than any you can ever press, Costa."

Guiseppe's face hardens, and his voice rises. "You don't understand how power works."

There is a beat of silence and then Andre, another one of the more powerful men in the family snorts, loud and derisive. "A woman leading us? Are you joking?" He stands, the scrape of his chair loud in the tense quiet. "This isn't how things are done, Angelo. You think parading Carlo's daughter in front of us is enough to keep this family together?"

"I'm not here because of tradition," Sophia says, her voice clear. "I'm here because I was born to lead this family. My father built it and his blood runs through my veins. That makes me the rightful heir. And as long as I'm standing, no one will take this family from me."

A few murmurs break out among the men, but Guiseppe's smirk only widens. He turns to the men around the table, spreading his arms as if to say, *do you believe this?*

"Women don't lead, Sophia. Women don't command respect—they don't inspire fear. Women belong..." he lets his words hang for a moment before continuing, his voice dripping with contempt. "...on their knees in front of their men. That's where they serve. With their mouths open. or in the kitchen."

Disgust and anger pull in my belly, and my palms ball into fists. It would be easy to pull out a gun and make sure Costa never utters another word again, but I agreed to play this her way.

"Not my wife, that woman cannot tell the difference between salt and baking soda. I think the bedroom is where they belong. To be seen, not heard," another man says, and laughs.

A few of his loyalists snicker, but the rest of the men are quiet, eyes darting between Sophia and me. Guiseppe has crossed a line, and he knew it. But this is his play—to provoke, to insult her publicly. To make her lose control.

Before I can react, Sophia speaks.

"You're all so backward you belong in the stone age." She shakes her head, walking straightening up.

She takes a step toward Guiseppe, meeting his eyes head-on. "It's funny how men like you always seem so afraid of women who can do things. Is it because you know you'll be crushed by us once you let us have our freedom?"

Guiseppe's smirk falters for just a second, but he recovers quickly. "I'm not afraid of you. I just don't take orders from women. And neither do the rest of us."

"I take orders from women," I say. "This organization depends on good leadership, no matter who offers it."

Sophia's eyes flash to mine, and she gives me a brief smile before turning away. "I'm not here to beg for your respect, Guiseppe. I'm here to take it. And if that means I have to teach you a lesson in humility, so be it."

His sneer returns. "Humility? And how exactly are you going to teach me about that?"

"The old-fashioned way," she replies smoothly. "You seem hell-bent on proving that I can't do anything you can do. I seem to remember that my father used a very simple method to figure out who belonged in his inner circle. Surely you remember this," she baits Costa, giving him a saucy wink.

I enjoy watching Costa squirm. Each time she brings up something from the past, something that only someone on the inside can know, it's another nail in his coffin.

"We'll engage in a contest. Outside. If I beat you, you'll keep your mouth shut, follow orders, and accept my leadership. If you win, we'll talk."

Guiseppe's eyebrows shoot up in surprise, but he doesn't back down. "What kind of contest?"

"Shooting," Sophia says, her voice cutting through the tension like a knife. "If you think you can handle a woman so easily, it should be no problem for you to beat me. After all, you're all worried I can't hold my own, that I'll be dead weight. Let me show you otherwise. The men who were the best shots were always at the heart of my father's inner circle. As someone who used to be his right-hand man, you should be able to prove that you earned the position fairly."

The room is silent. I can see the calculation in Guiseppe's eyes. He's arrogant enough to believe he can win, but the challenge itself caught him off guard. He hadn't expected her to push back, especially not like this.

After a moment, Guiseppe's lips curl into a twisted smile. "Fine," he says. "But don't start crying when you lose, sweetheart."

Sophia doesn't react. "Lead the way," she says, gesturing toward the door.

The sun hangs low as we step into the yard behind the estate, into a stretch of open space that Carlo had used for similar tests of loyalty. The tension follows us outside. It's palpable as all the men file out to watch.

Guiseppe swaggers forward, his arrogance practically oozing off him as he grabs a handgun from one of the men. Sophia accepts her own without a word as I pass it to her, checking the weight in her hands as though she's done this a hundred times. Maybe she has—there is still a lot about Sophia's past she hasn't shared with me.

"Put the targets on the wall," Guiseppe barks, his voice full of swagger as the men set up the paper markers that indicate the silhouette of a person's head and shoulders.

Sophia aims at the target, hefting the gun, shifting it in her hand, her focus never wavering. Guiseppe steps up beside her, still smirking. "Ladies first."

Without missing a beat, Sophia fires. The shot drills right through the center of the head on the target. Before anyone can blink, she fires again, delivering another bullet to precisely the same spot. The silence that follows is deafening.

I see the flicker of doubt that crosses Guiseppe's face, but he quickly masks it. "Not bad for a woman," he mutters, lifting his gun.

He fires once, clipping the edge of the paper target. His face flushes as he readjusts, lining up for his second shot. This time, he hits the target near the center of the silhouette's head.

"I believe the next phase was walking backward and shooting at the target," Sophia says, and no sooner has she spoken, than she starts pacing backward. She delivers two more shots near the center of the target's head, then glances over at Guiseppe.

"This is an excellent display," he sneers. "How long did you have to practice to be able to put on this little show?"

Sophia laughs bitterly. "Oh, I assure you that this is not a party trick I have perfected. The life of a child of a great Cosa Nostra leader is rife with danger. I was raised to protect myself and I took the assignment very seriously. But you wouldn't know about that, having come from a secondary family, and only having been in the wings of power your whole life."

I see the rage flare across his face before he manages to shove it away. He's breathing hard as he starts walking backward, his nostrils pinched and his mouth a harsh line. I hear murmuring among the men at Sophia's words.

Guiseppe's first shot hits the target, but down by the shoulders. The next shot barely punctures the edge of the top of the head. He stares at the evidence of his poor marksmanship, something dangerous hiding in his dark eyes.

Sophia looks at Guiseppe with her arms crossed. She puts the safety back on and passes the handgun back to me. "Looks like you lost," she says. "Seems that women can defend themselves, after all, if you let them have the training necessary to do so."

She turns to look at the group of assembled men. "I dare anyone else to step up and show me that they can do better than me."

There's a heavy silence, punctuated only by the sound of Costa's rough breathing.

She looks around at the gathering. "Come on now," she baits them. "No one else wants to prove that women are only good for childbirth and blowjobs?"

The tension snaps back into the air, thicker than before. Guiseppe's jaw clenches, but before he can say anything, I step forward. "A deal's a deal, Costa. You lost. And now, you'll respect her leadership or find your way out."

Guiseppe glares at me. There is something dangerous behind his eyes. "This isn't over, Angelo. You may have burned my crates and tried to shame me, but you haven't won."

The men shift uneasily. They all know about Costa's smuggling operation—and they know I burned his shipment as retaliation for his attack on Luca. But Costa isn't just angry about the money. This is personal now.

"I'll tell you this once," I say softly, stepping closer. "Talk about Sophia like that again, and I'll make sure you leave here in pieces. Understood?"

Guiseppe's sneer doesn't disappear, but he gives a curt nod. He isn't stupid. He knows the threat is real.

I turn back to the group. "Sophia Agostini is the leader of this family. And there's one more thing." I look at Sophia, a slight smile tugging at my lips. "We're engaged. We are honoring the contract that my father and Carlo made years ago. They intended that we would bind our families and Sophia and I are honoring that demand."

The shock ripples through the crowd like a wave. Guiseppe is the first to react, his voice filled with venom.

"Engaged? This is all a power play, then. You're using her to gain control of the Agostini family."

"Say what you like," I reply coolly. "But you'll follow her, or you'll deal with me."

Sophia steps forward again, her voice steady and sharp. "We may be engaged, but don't think for a second that our engagement is intended to thwart you, Guiseppe. This family is mine. You'll either fall in line or fall off the map."

Her words hang heavy in the air as Guiseppe turns on his heel and storms off, his followers reluctantly trailing after him. The rest of the men linger, their expressions worried as they process what just happened.

One by one, they nod in respect to Sophia, acknowledging her as the new leader.

Chapter Fourteen

Sophia

The sound of the shots I fired rings in my ears long after the contest has ended. I can still feel the weight of the gun in my hands, the recoil, the cold satisfaction that settled in my chest when Guiseppe missed his first shot. This wasn't about proving him wrong. This wasn't even about winning. It was about survival.

I'd stood in front of the men who had once followed my father and demanded they follow me. And they had. Well, most of them. For now, that was enough.

But the real victory came when I saw the flash of fear in Guiseppe's eyes, even if he tried to mask it with arrogance. He'd underestimated me. They all had.

I stand in front of the full-length mirror in my room, staring at my reflection. I don't recognize the woman looking back at me. There's a sharpness in her eyes that wasn't there before, a hardness that I'm not sure I like. But this is who I have to be now.

My mother had always warned me, "Never let them see the cracks". But cracks were inevitable when you were holding this much weight on your shoulders.

I glance at the engagement ring Angelo had slipped onto my finger earlier. It feels foreign on my hand, like it doesn't belong to me, a symbol of a life I haven't chosen. And yet here I was, wearing it, playing a part I don't fully understand yet.

I feel faint suddenly, and I press and hand to my chest. I sit down clumsily in the chair near the mirror, the room spinning a little as I try and collect myself. My stomach turns a bit and I hunch forward, closing my eyes.

What's wrong with me? Is this some kind of delayed reaction to the stress of the day?

I hunch over and wait for the wave of discomfort to pass. It's been a stressful few weeks. Surely that is all that is wrong with me.

A knock at the door pulls me out of my thoughts. I already know who it will be. Feeling slightly less peaked, I rise cautiously and go to open the door.

Angelo stands in the doorway, his expression unreadable as always, but his eyes...they soften when they landed on me. It's subtle, but I've spent enough time around him now to know his tells. There's something comforting in that, even if I'm not ready to admit it.

"How are you holding up?" he asks, stepping into the room and closing the door behind him.

I let out a breath I didn't realize I'd been holding. "I'm fine. That went...better than I expected."

"You did better than they expected," he corrects, his voice low, his gaze lingering on me for a moment too long. "You handled yourself well."

The compliment feels strange coming from him. I wasn't supposed to care what he thought. But I did. Maybe too much.

"All those years in the shooting club, all the competitions," I say, shaking my head. "I thought my mother was just promoting interests that our wealthy friends enjoyed." My mouth twists a little. "Turns out she was making sure that I could protect myself."

"She was a wise woman," Angelo says.

I nod, and pace away to look out the window. I can't think of my mother. Not right now. The thought of her feels like holding my hand too close to an open flame. At a certain distance, the thought is comforting and brings joy, but the moment my fingers move too close, the pain is there, sharp, staggering and permanent.

"Costa's not done," I say, avoiding the weight of Angelo's stare by turning toward the window. The city skyline stretches out before me, a reminder of how far I am from the life my mother and I built. "He's going to come at me harder next time."

"I'll handle Costa," Angelo replies, his voice taking on that hard edge I'd come to recognize. "You don't need to worry about him."

I turn to face him, my frustration bubbling to the surface. "That's the problem, Angelo. I'm not here for you to handle things for me. I can't lead this family if you keep swooping in every time someone threatens me."

His jaw clenches, but he doesn't argue. Instead, he steps closer, his hand brushing against my arm, a touch that sends a shiver down my spine. "You're right. But you're not alone in this. You don't have to be."

There it is again—the softness, the vulnerability he tries so hard to hide. And it's always moments like this that make it harder to keep my walls up. I want to believe him. I want to let him shoulder the weight with me. But I can't shake the feeling that letting him in means losing some of myself in the process.

"I'm not used to relying on anyone," I say quietly, my voice barely above a whisper. "I've spent my whole life running, taking care of myself, handling things on my own. It's hard to just...let that go."

His hand slides down to my wrist, his fingers wrapping around it in a way that isn't possessive, but grounding. "You don't have to let it go, Sophia. Just don't carry it all alone."

I close my eyes, letting his words sink in. There's a part of me that wants to fight him on this, to push him away. But the truth is, I'm exhausted. I've been carrying this burden—this fear—for too long. And for the first time in a long time, someone is offering to share it with me.

When I open my eyes again, he's still watching me, his gaze intense but gentle. And in that moment, I make a decision.

I step forward, closing the space between us. "I don't want to be alone anymore."

The words come out before I can stop them, and I see the flash of surprise in his eyes. But it is quickly replaced by something else—something darker, more primal.

His hands move to my waist, pulling me closer, his body heat seeping into mine. "You won't be," he murmurs, his breath hot against my skin.

I reach up, my fingers threading through the hair at the nape of his neck, pulling him down to me. His lips meet mine in a kiss that isn't gentle, isn't soft. It's fierce, demanding, filled with all the things we haven't said, the things we can't say.

His hands are everywhere, sliding under my shirt, gripping my waist, pulling me closer until there's no space left between us. His kiss is bruising, and I give as good as I get, my fingers clawing at his shirt, desperate to feel more of him.

"Angelo," I breathe, his name a plea on my lips as his mouth moves to my neck, his teeth grazing my skin in a way that makes my knees weak.

He doesn't say anything, just presses me harder against the wall, his hands slipping under my waistband, tugging at the fabric until it slides down my legs.

I tug at his belt, and he curses under his breath, his hands working in tandem with mine until his pants hit the floor. He lifts me, and I wrap my legs around his waist, gasping as he pushes inside me in one swift motion.

There's no gentleness between us, no hesitation. We move together with a raw, desperate intensity, each thrust pulling us deeper into the storm of our emotions.

I moan into his mouth, my fingers digging into his shoulders as he drives me closer and closer to the edge. His lips are on my neck, my shoulder, his breath hot and ragged against my skin.

"Fuck, Sophia," he groans, his voice thick with need as he buries himself deeper inside me.

I cling to him, my body trembling as the pleasure builds to an unbearable peak. And when it finally crashes over me, I shatter in his arms, my head falling back as I cry out his name.

Angelo follows me over the edge, his body tensing as he finds his release, his arms tightening around me as though he can't bear to let me go.

For a long moment, we stay like that, our bodies pressed together, our breath mingling in the quiet aftermath of the storm. And for the first time since this whole nightmare began, I feel something other than fear.

I feel...safe.

Later, I lie in bed, staring up at the ceiling as the events of the day replay in my mind. The contest with Guiseppe, the engagement announcement, and the way Angelo's touch burned away the tension in my chest.

But the calm is temporary. I know that. Guiseppe isn't done, and neither are the men who still doubt me. This victory is only the first of many battles I'll have to fight to keep control of the Agostini family.

But I wasn't the same woman who'd arrived in New York, terrified and unsure of her place. I had proven myself today. And I would prove myself again.

I turn to look at Angelo, his face relaxed in sleep beside me. His presence, once something I'd resented, has become something else. Something I'm not sure I want to define yet. But I know one thing—he's right. I don't have to carry this burden alone anymore.

And maybe, just maybe, that isn't such a bad thing.

***

I pace the room, glancing out at the city that stretches out far below the penthouse. It should feel so foreign—New York, this world, the role I'm now playing. But it doesn't. It scares me that this all feels so natural to me.

The engagement ring on my finger feels heavier than it should, the metal cool and unfamiliar against my skin. Fake engagement, real consequences. Angelo had announced it like it was no big deal, but the ripple effect was already happening.

I could feel the shift among the men, the way they watched me more closely. I was sure that some of them were calculating, waiting to see if I could hold my ground. Others, like Costa, were biding their time, waiting for me to slip up.

Vertigo washes over me, and I put a hand against the window frame to steady myself. The spells of discomfort have been getting worse over the past couple of days.

I swallow heavily, tasting bile in my throat. I whirl abruptly, running to the bathroom to slump over the toilet, violently sick.

Maybe I'm getting the flu. I lean back against the tub, feeling shaky and spent. This is all I need. Being sick when I'm in the throes of taking over my father's empire is not ideal.

I wasn't sure how long I had been crumpled on the bathroom floor when I heard Justine's voice echoing down the hall. I straighten up with effort forcing myself to breathe deeply. My stomach still felt questionable and my head didn't feel like it was attached to my shoulders.

"Sarah!" Justine's voice is a sing-song chant as she enters the room, her usual grin firmly in place. Of course, she hadn't switched to calling me Sophia yet. To her, I was still the girl she'd grown up with, not some mafia princess.

She frowns when she sees me curled up on the bathroom floor. "Oh, love," she says, rushing to my side. "What's wrong?"

I shake my head. "I don't know. I've been feeling sick on and off for a few days now."

"Well, we can't have that," Justine says. "I'll make you some tea. If I can find the kitchen in this palatial apartment."

I smile a little. Tea was the British way of solving everything. Bit tired in the morning? Have some tea. Your favorite football team lost a game? Have some tea. You're sick as a dog and have to take over a mafia family? Have some tea.

"I don't need tea, but thank you," I say to her, my voice thin. I idly swing open the cabinet under the sink. "Maybe I'm just about to start my period," I muse. "Sometimes I feel icky the couple of days before."

Justine gives me a stern look. "Not like this," she insists. "Let me make you some tea. You'll feel better as soon as you've had a few sips."

"Are there tampons in any of those cabinets?" I ask her, ignoring her advice.

She rolls her eyes and starts rummaging through the fancy bathroom.

"Nope," she says with a little shake of her head. "Angelo seems to think of everything. Maybe he forgot you were a real, human woman."

I gave her a tight smile. "Trust me, this isn't exactly how either of us pictured things."

"Oh, come on," she teased, resting her chin on her hands. "Living in a mansion with a big, brooding man who is obsessed with you? It's pretty terrible, you're right."

I giggle with her, despite how terrible I feel.

"And, dear God, have you seen Franco? What's in the water here? It's ridiculous."

Her eyes sparkle, but I can see the questions bubbling just beneath the surface.

"It's not exactly a fairy tale, Jus," I say "None of this is. This engagement...it's not what it looks like."

She tilts her head, her smile faltering for the first time since she'd arrived. "What do you mean?"

I take a deep breath, staring at the ring for a second before slipping it off my finger and dropping it onto the floor between us. The metal clinks softly against the wood and Justine's eyes widen in surprise. "It's fake," I say, shrugging. "All of it. The engagement, the relationship—everything."

"What?" she straightens up, her brows pulling together in confusion. "But why? Angelo…he seems…"

I shake my head. "It's complicated. Angelo's using the engagement to solidify my place in the family, to make sure no one questions my leadership. But it's all just part of the plan. Nothing is real."

Justine is quiet for a moment, her gaze fixed on the ring. "And you're okay with that?"

"Doesn't matter if I am or not," I reply, my voice harder than I intend it to be. "It's what I have to do. If this is what keeps me alive—keeps us alive—then I don't have a choice."

There's a long pause before Justine sighs. "I get it," she says softly, her teasing gone. "But still, it's shit, isn't it? Living a lie."

I nod, my throat tightening. "It is."

Suddenly, I know I'm going to be sick again and I lunge toward the toilet, barely managing to throw up without making a huge mess.

I hear the sink running, and then Justine is pressing a cool hand towel to my forehead. She tsks softly as she helps me lean back against the wall again.

"Babe," she says to me gently, "what if you don't need tampons?"

I crack one eye open and look up at her in confusion. "What?" I manage to croak.

She's giving me a sad, motherly look and I feel alarm tighten my insides.

"How long have you been here in New York?"

I do some quick math. "I don't know, about four weeks?"

She looks down at the floor for a moment, then meets my gaze again. "Have you been sleeping with Angelo the whole time you've been here?"

I feel like a boulder has been dropped into my stomach.

"Oh my God," I whisper, pressing a hand to my belly. "But, I've been taking my pills."

"On time?" she asks me.

I wince. "I mean, mostly," I admit. I close my eyes and lean my head back against the wall. This cannot be happening.

"Well," Justine says, "these things do happen, even when people are on the pill."

I feel a tear slip down my cheek. This is not how I wanted to find out I was pregnant. This is not how I wanted to become a mother.

"Let me have Franco take me to get some tests. Or maybe I can send him out for us." She giggles.

I grab her hand before she can move. "No!" I cry out, making her stop abruptly. "No, you can't do that. No one can know."

She frowns at me, confused. "Babe, we need to know if you really are pregnant. You need to stop taking the pill, you need to go see a doctor…"

I shake my head, despite how it makes my nausea ratchet up. "No, Justine, we cannot, must not, do that. No one can know about this. It will make me seem weak, vulnerable, like I can be taken down. And," I grimace as a new thought occurs to me, "everyone will want to kidnap our child to try to force Angelo's hand, or even my hand."

Justine sighs, coming to sit down next to me. "Well, fuck," she says.

I laugh despite the fear coiled within me. "Indeed," I agree.

She takes my hand, squeezing it. "We've kept secrets before," she says softly.

I look over at her and meet her gaze. There are tears standing in her eyes and I feel my own eyes prickly with moisture.

"Yes," I whisper.

"I'm going to be the best auntie ever!" she whispers fiercely before a tear slides down her cheek.

We share a sisterly smile, and she leans over to hug me.

As we pull apart, I realize that I'm feeling a little better. "I think I want that tea now," I tell her.

Justine smiles primly at me. "If you would have just let me get you some to start with you would have been right as rain by now.

I laughed, rolling my eyes. "Yeah, yeah," I tell her.

We walk toward the kitchen, Justine prattling on about the handsome mafia men all over the place and how she wants to see the museums in the city.

"Please, Jus, don't start with Franco," I plead at one point as I rummage through the kitchen looking for tea.

"Oh, once I've started, you know I can't stop." She winks at me "I'm not blind, babe. I saw the way he looked at me when I got here. He's stoic, brooding, completely infuriating... but hot as hell. And I like a challenge."

"I don't think Franco is the type to..."

"To what? Be swayed by my undeniable charm?" she shoots me a grin as she grabs some mugs from a shelf. "Watch me work my magic."

I sigh. Justine is incorrigible, but I'm glad she's here. I know she still has no idea what we are up against. And as much as I want to believe her words, this isn't a game I can win with a little charm.

The weight of the situation settles back on my shoulders as we sip our tea. The house is too quiet. It's the kind of silence that makes you think too much—the kind of silence that makes you question everything.

I glance over at Justine, opening my mouth to say something to her, when I realize that she's scrolling through the Instacart app on her phone.

"What are you doing?" I ask her.

"Just a minute," she says distractedly. "This looks so different than the version we have in the UK," she mutters, scrolling quickly.

I watch her type in payment info and hit confirm before she turns to grin at me.

"What are you up to?" I ask her.

"Solving a problem for you. I have a delivery arriving in about an hour," she says with a grin. "No need to tell anyone about our little secret due to the magic of technology."

"You ordered?" I start to say, then fall silent as Franco wanders into the kitchen.

"What are you two whispering about?" he asks us, but there's a smile nestled into the corner of his lips.

"Oh, you know, just having a little hen do here in the kitchen," Justine says, her accent front and center.

"A hen...what?" he repeats, looking genuinely confused.

We both laugh. "A hen do is a bachelorette party in the UK," I explain. "But sometimes it's used as a bit of a joke about when women are gathered together gossiping and stuff."

Franco shakes his head. "You English are strange folk."

"You mean sexy folk," Justine says with a sultry smile.

I tune them out as they banter back and forth, worrying over the idea of being pregnant. I don't even know how I feel about such a thing coming to pass. I had never actually even considered having children. I had been too scared of exposing them to the risk that my mother and I lived with every day.

But it didn't matter now. If I was actually pregnant, then all of those desires, worries, or concerns didn't really matter anymore. Now I would have to figure out what to do about this new life. How would I protect it? Would I tell Angelo? Would I keep it?

As soon as I think about any option other than keeping my baby, my mind immediately rejects that choice. There is no way that I'm not going to have this baby.

"Oh! My delivery is here!" Justine announces abruptly. "I'll just pop down and make sure I grab it, then I'll be back."

Franco and I watch her leave. My heart is pounding in my chest. Now that I can find out the truth, I feel terrified.

Franco gets a call and leaves the room. I sigh in relief. I don't think that I can hide my panic for much longer. It feels like Justine hasn't been gone for even a moment before she shows back up with a plastic drugstore bag in her hand.

She looks around, sees that Franco is gone, and gestures for me to follow her. Like a sleepwalker, I go with her into my bedroom.

She's talking about how to take the tests, and saying she got three, just to be safe. Her words wash over me. I feel nothing as I take the tests. Even the tips of my fingers are numb.

We wait for the little window to reveal the truth I'm dreading. The minutes tick by, slow and torturous.

When the results appear, I stare at them, my stomach lurching.

Pregnant.

For a moment, everything is still. The world stops spinning and all I can hear is the sound of my own breathing, too fast, too shallow. This wasn't part of the plan. This changes everything. Justine's hands come to rest on my shoulders.

"I know," she says soothingly, stroking my hair back from my face. "But it's going to be okay. You've handled everything else so far. You'll handle this, too."

I press my hand against my abdomen, the reality of it sinking in. A baby. Angelo's baby.

Fuck.

Chapter Fifteen

Angelo

Those girls are thick as thieves.

I stare at Franco's text and shake my head. Did he expect anything else? Women who grew up together tended to be as close as sisters. I was glad that Sophia had Justine here with her, supporting her, but I'm also worried about her presence. Franco can't keep an eye on them both all day long. He has other duties to take care of as well.

I dismiss these thoughts. I don't have time to worry about anyone other than myself and my men right now. A small group of my most loyal men and I are driving into Guiseppe's territory, on our way to a meeting with an inside man we planted months ago. We need to extract him now that Costa is on to us.

We drive into a shady part of the warehouse district, my heart feeling pinched in my chest. Guiseppe is capable of nearly anything and I hate being on his side of the fence. I don't want to stay here for a moment longer than necessary.

We drive to the agreed-upon meeting location and park against the side of a warehouse that is barely still standing. I pull out my gun, letting it rest on my thigh as I look out the tinted window.

"No sign of him yet," the man in the driver's seat says quietly.

I don't bother to answer. My nerves are strung tight, my heart pounding. I feel like something might go wrong, but I have no idea why. I have learned to trust my instincts, however, and when I have a bad feeling, I listen to it.

Suddenly, there's commotion, the noise of vehicles and what sounds like a motorcycle. I sit up straighter in my seat, turning off the safety on my gun.

The motorcycle I thought I heard, tears around the corner and I see that my spy is clinging to the side of the tank awkwardly. He leaps from the bike, allowing it to slide along the asphalt and fetch up against the wall with a crash.

I whip the car door open and practically catch the man as he falls into my arms. There's so much blood. I barely recognize the man as I drag him back toward the car. He's trying to speak, but I can't understand anything he's saying. My stomach turns over as I realize why there's so much blood and why I can't understand a word he's saying.

Costa cut his tongue out.

Two black SUVs whip around the corner and men boil out of them. They don't ask questions before they start shooting. I take a moment to fire my gun at them, wanting only to distract them as I shove my man into the car and scramble in behind him.

"Go!" I shout, grappling with the open car door as my driver takes off. Bullets ring against the sides of the car as tires squeal. I lose a hold of the car door, and slide across the seat as we turn in a sharp circle. I manage to catch myself as I start to fall out of the car, but the door slams shut on my hand.

"Fuck!" I bellow, yanking my hand from the door. We turn and swerve around another corner, and the door shuts on its own, latching this time. I cradle my hand in my lap, feeling nauseous.

"You all right, boss?" the man in the passenger seat asks me.

I stifle another curse. "Yeah. Broke my hand," I say. I look over at my informant. His eyes are wild in his face, but he's still alive. For now.

"Call Doc," I say to the man in the passenger seat. "Gianni needs him immediately."

"Where to?" the driver asks me, swerving around another corner.

I look behind us and don't see either of Guiseppe's SUVs following us.

"Gianni can't wait for help," I say. "We need to go to my place. It's close."

"Boss, don't you think that.." the man in the front seat says.

"You heard me," I snap. I pull my phone out of my pocket and dial Franco's number awkwardly with my good hand.

"Yep?" Franco says as he picks up the call.

"Nine-one-one," I say to him, sucking a breath in between my clenched teeth as my hand throbs painfully. "We're coming to you. Doc's on his way."

"How bad?" Franco asks, his voice hard.

"Very," I say and disconnect the call.

I look over my shoulder. Still no tail. It doesn't really surprise me. Guiseppe did this to send a message. He isn't interested in chasing me across the city.

Thankfully, there isn't much traffic and it only takes a few more minutes before we arrive at my building. The driver pulls into the underground garage and I leap out before the car even stops moving. Gianni is slumped against the door, and when I open the door, he spills limply into my arms.

"There's so much blood," I hear someone say.

"A little help here?" I snap, trying to balance Gianni with one hand.

"You dumb bastards! Don't just stare. Help the boss out."

I look over my shoulder and see that Franco has arrived. I know him well enough to see his shock at the sight of Gianni and me covered in blood.

"What the fuck," he mutters. "Are you all right?" he asks me, helping to support Gianni's weight as we start to take him toward the elevator.

"Mostly," I say. "It's all his blood. They cut out his tongue."

"The fuck," Franco growls. "Animals."

The ride up to the penthouse feels like it's taking hours. I awkwardly press my finger to the fingerprint scanner that gives the elevator permission to go up to the top floor. As soon as the elevator pings, we all spill out, a trail of blood slicking the floor.

"Where's Doc?" I demand as my men carry Gianni into the kitchen. They lift him onto the large kitchen island, and Franco hurries to the pantry to get out the huge first-aid kit that I keep in there for situations just like this one.

"He's downstairs. He's on his way up," Franco says from the pantry. He comes out with the first-aid box in his hand.

"What's going on?"

I look over my shoulder and see Justine and Sophia rushing into the kitchen. Justine claps a hand over her mouth at the sight of all the blood. She stands still for a moment, then races out of the room, no doubt to be sick.

Sophia, however, wades into the mess without a qualm. "Let me help," she says commandingly. "Give me some gauze."

I step back, holding my aching hand. She will be of far more use than myself with my broken hand. I feel a swoop of lightheadedness and lean back against the counter.

I have seen a lot of terrible things, but this...this is something else. It's a level of brutality that I never expected from Costa. Honestly, it's a level of brutality that I have only ever heard old mafia men talk about.

"What've we got?"

I look up and see Doc wading into the group of people attending to Gianni on the kitchen counter. He slips a little in the blood on the floor but catches himself before he goes down.

Doc has been our personal doctor ever since I was a young man. He's about ten years older than me, sharp as a tack and completely trustworthy. He's actually a plastic surgeon with his own private clinic, but he knows his way around emergency medicine.

We pay him well to be on-call at all times. His father was one of my father's most trusted men, so he grew up in the life. He understands what we need and he provides it with unflagging commitment.

We've even used his day job skills from time to time to send men into hiding. He's very good at what he does.

"Costa," I say. "Cut his tongue out."

"Fucking bastard," Doc says savagely. He tilts Gianni's head to the side, and peers into his mouth.

"Do we need to get him to the clinic?" I ask.

"Yes, but I need to get this bleeding in order first. Give me a few minutes to keep him from bleeding out."

I watch Doc working quickly and efficiently, his blue eyes trained on the man on the counter with intense focus.

"You're new here," Doc says to Sophia as he struggles to Gianni's mouth to stop bleeding.

She hands him more gauze and helps steady the man's head. "Sophia Agostini," she says matter-of-factly.

He glances up sharply at her for a beat. "Royalty among us," he comments.

She snorts, swiping her hair back away from her face. She leaves a smear of Gianni's blood across her forehead. "Hardly," she says back. "Mostly, I'm just a liability around here."

"Agree to disagree," Doc says back. "Alessio Ricci. Doc to the stars...and Angelo Castiglia's family."

Sophia smiles at him for a beat. "Glad to meet you."

"What's wrong with your hand?" Doc says to me distractedly as he continues to work.

I sigh. "Broke it. Car door slammed on it as we got away."

Sophia looks over her shoulder at me. "Shit," she says. She sounds annoyed and I grin. I love when she's bossy. I love seeing her act like a don.

"Agreed," I say.

"You should come to the clinic later," Doc says. He steps back from Gianni, then gestures to the men hovering at the edge of the room to pick him up and take him to the elevator. "I can take a couple of X-rays and get you fixed up."

I shake my head. "I'll just go to the ER," I say. "It's not a big deal."

"Your choice," Doc says. "You know I don't mind." He nods at Sophia, and she inclines her head in reply. We watch him hustle after the group of my men who are carrying Gianni's unconscious body to the elevator.

"Will he be okay?"

We both glance over and see Justine hovering in the doorway of Sophia's bedroom. She's white as a sheet.

I lift a shoulder in a shrug. "I hope so. Doc's great at what he does. He couldn't be in better hands, but it's a terrible injury."

Sophia utters a string of harsh curses, staring down at her bloody hands. She jerks into motion and grabs a roll of paper towels to start soaking up the blood that is everywhere. I realize that I should help and I gesture to her to pass me the roll so that I can help out.

"Why the fuck would anyone do something like that?" Justine says. Her voice is hoarse and I can barely hear her.

"Guiseppe is a bastard who will stop at nothing to steal my legacy," Sophia says snappishly as she jerkily soaks up the blood with the paper towels. "He's trying to scare me...us."

"Well, it's working," Justine says softly. She wraps her arms around herself as if she's cold.

Sophia looks over her shoulder and something seems to unravel within her. Her expression softens as she looks at her friend.

"We should send you back home," she says to Justine. "You don't belong here. You shouldn't be tangled up in this."

"Neither should you!" Justine says, suddenly angry. She glares at me and I feel a twist of regret in my chest. She's not wrong, really. Sophia should be safely living her life as Sarah Lacey in England, going to the pub with Justine, watching football matches, riding the tube to work each day. She shouldn't be caught up in any of this.

"You should both go," I hear myself say. I hadn't planned to say it, but it's the truth. Neither of them deserve this. "I can get you both on a flight to the UK within a few hours. You can go back to your lives."

Sophia shakes her head. "I'm not going anywhere, Angelo. I don't disagree that Justine should go home, but what in the actual hell do you think I will do in the UK? You think they won't find me? You think they won't track me down to try to get to you?"

I wince. She's not wrong and I hate that she's making sense. I brought her into this mess. I made her come home to take her rightful place in her father's seat.

It just never occurred to me that Guiseppe would handle her presence like this. I had known he was a bad man, but I would have never expected him to be willing to go so far just to scare Sophia into submission and to make me realize that he meant business.

Two of my men, maimed beyond repair. Two bold, aggressive and horrifying statements. I honestly wanted to crawl into a hole and hide, but Sophia seemed ready and willing to fight tooth and nail to stop him. I wonder where she's getting her strength from. I'm envious of it at the moment.

"If Sophia's staying, I'm staying too," Justine says, joining us in the kitchen. She starts helping clean up the mess. She's still a bit green around the gills, but she has spunk, I'll give her that.

"I told you that this would happen," Franco says as he steps out of the elevator. He brushes past me to go wash his hands at the sink. He looks down at his slacks, which are stained with Gianni's blood and he frowns.

"I know," I say. He hadn't predicted Guiseppe would go to such lengths, but he had predicted that things would be ugly. I hadn't listened. I had just gone to fetch Sophia as if this would all be a cakewalk.

"You need to step things up," Franco says abruptly as he turns to look at me again.

"What?" I say, confused.

"You two need to get married, and fast," he repeats. "Guiseppe's ability to hit us where it counts is going to start making waves. We can't afford to take chances with anything now. If you two get married, the consequences of killing either of you escalate. The decision to harm either of you when you are married would mean an all-out war. It would call in reinforcements and demand that allies unite."

Sophia has gone very still, her gaze on my face, but her entire being turned inward. I don't know what she's thinking. It could be good, or bad, or it could be nothing.

"Goddammit," she says quietly, pinching the bridge of her nose with her fingers.

"We don't have to do that," I say. "At least not for real. We can pretend, say we got married, but not do anything official. You don't have to be stuck here."

Sophia is still standing in front of me with her eyes closed. She finally opens them and her expression is stark, hopeless. I hate seeing her like this. I hate my part in all of this.

"You don't get it," she says, her voice sounding like dry leaves rattling down the New York streets. "This," she waves her hand at the remnants of the mess in the kitchen, "this happened because of me. All of the bad things that are happening are because of me. I can't just run away and hide, and I don't have any choice about marrying you if I stay. The only way I can make this right is to marry you, whether I want to or not."

Whether I want to or not. The words sting. I know I should be able to divorce fact from fiction. I know that I told her this was all just a temporary game we were playing until her father's legacy was secured. But somehow, somewhere along the way, I've realized that I'm falling for her, that I want more.

The realization washes over me in a wave. I want romance with this woman. I want her to fall in love with me, to be thrilled on her wedding day as she walks down the aisle toward me. I want her to get to plan the perfect mafia princess wedding, to invite all of her friends to come see us get hitched.

I don't want her to choose me out of necessity, because our fathers forced us together. I don't want a bride who is marrying me at gunpoint.

I want her to love me the way that I have come to love her.

"Can the...Doc...help you escape?" Justine says, her voice trembling a little. She looks between us, her skin so pale that she looks like a beautiful specter standing in the kitchen in front of us.

"He could," I agree, although the thought of someone changing her face, altering her beauty makes me sick inside.

She shakes her head firmly. "No," she says. "All I have left of my parents is my father's business and my mother's face. I'm not changing any of it. I'm facing it. I'm claiming it. They are both mine, and goddammit, I'm not letting some gutter shite try and take it from me."

I blink a little at the cockney phrase rolling off her tongue. I look over at Justine and she's smiling a little. Franco is even giving her an approving look.

"I'll let you two sort out the details of all of this," Franco says. "I need to take the Maid of Honor to her place to get some sleep." He gestures to Justine, and she floats over to him, allowing him to place his arm over her shoulders and guide her toward the elevator.

I watch them vanish into the elevator, headed down to her apartment, and then I turn to Sophia.

"You don't have to do anything you don't want to do," I tell her again. "We can figure something out that doesn't involve you staying here, being exposed to all this danger."

Sophia gives me a hard look. "Here's the thing," she says. "A few weeks ago, I would have given anything to avoid all of this, to avoid coming back here. But now," she looks around at the messy kitchen, then down at her blood-encrusted nails, "now it's like there's a fire burning in me, like my heart is made of hot coals. I want him to *pay* for this. I want to secure what's mine...and yours, for so many reasons."

She presses her hand to her belly, looking down at her fingers. I see her breaths lifting her shoulders ever so slightly as she gathers herself, steadies herself.

"If you want this, I will help you to the best of my ability," I promise her. There are so many other things I want to say. I want to speak of love, duty, and commitment, but I can't, not now. None of the affection that I feel for her is helpful right now. Maybe it won't ever be.

"Thank you," she says, still looking down at her hand pressed to her flat stomach. "This is going to be a tough fight. When should we get married?"

"I can get someone to marry us tomorrow if you want," I say.

She nods. "Do it," she says, then turns away and goes to her room.

Chapter Sixteen

Sophia

"You look beautiful," Justine says to me, fussing over my long hair, which she has been putting into an updo.

I look at my reflection. I'm pale, but the lack of color in my skin somehow makes me look starkly attractive paired with the lacy, white wedding dress that Justine and Franco somehow tracked down this morning.

My morning sickness has taken a break for the day, which is a blessing. I can't imagine anything worse than having to run to the bathroom to vomit in the middle of the wedding ceremony. A shotgun wedding ceremony would never be improved by a puking bride.

"Are you sure about all of this?" Justine asks me. Her color is back today and I think that her renewed calm has something to do with Franco. He stayed with her all night last night. I hope he helped her to forget the horror of yesterday with some affection.

"No," I say honestly. "But there's nothing else that makes sense. I have to do this, whether I want to or not. I have to see this through, for all of us. I'm the only one who can keep us all safe."

"But do you *want* it?" she asks me, meeting my gaze in the mirror.

I know what she's asking. Do I want Angelo? Do I want to lead the Agostini family?

The truth is that I think that I do, much to my surprise. I hate how this is all unfolding, hate that we are in danger, hate that I have to fight tooth and nail to assume my birthright.

But I still *want* all of it. I think I actually *want* to be the don of my family, and I know, with every fiber of my being, that I want Angelo. Just the sight of him this morning in the kitchen with his hand in a splint, his hair a mess, sipping his coffee, made me ache with longing.

For some reason, I don't feel alone when I'm with him. Justine is the only other person who has ever been able to fill that gap for me. The fact that Angelo makes me feel seen and loved is a rare gift. I know I would be foolish to throw that away.

"I do want it," I tell her. "All of it. Even the horrible parts. I don't know what that means about me."

Justine smiles softly. "It means you're a tough cookie," she says fondly, leaning over my shoulder to press a kiss to my cheek. "I'm proud of you."

I feel a bit warmer hearing her praise. I put on some lipstick as Justine finishes her work on my hair.

"Are you going to tell Angelo about...you know?" Justine says to me, stepping back to look at her work.

"I have to, I know," I say with a sigh. "But I want it to be the right time before I do. We have so much to worry about right now. There's no room for one more worry. And I need to be able to do my job. No one will take me seriously if I'm pregnant, Justine."

"I hate all the big-dick energy crap around here," Justine says tartly, and I giggle. "Well, I do!" she insists.

"You did wonder over and over what was in the water around here," I chide her.

"Big dick energy?" she says with a laugh. "Maybe that *is* what makes them all hot...and so scared of women."

"What about Franco?" I ask her carefully, rising from my spot in front of the mirror and wandering carefully across the room to put on my shoes. Thankfully I owned a variety of white heels that were all perfect for an impromptu wedding.

She's quiet for a moment and when I look over my shoulder at her, she's decidedly pink. "Big dick, eh?" I quip and she dissolves into giggles.

"And how," she agrees, pressing a hand to her mouth as she stifles her laughter.

I roll my eyes. "Well, I'm glad you weren't disappointed," I say.

She shakes her head. "Not at all, but it's more than that," she tells me. "He's so kind. I know he doesn't seem that way, but he has a heart of gold hiding under all that bravado."

A couple of weeks ago, I would have argued with her about this, but I realize that she's right. Franco has been willing to take care of both myself and Justine for weeks now, and he hasn't complained or shirked his duties. I know he has other things to do with his time, but he's always around when we need him, always eager to do what is necessary.

And his loyalty to Angelo is important to me as well. I know all too well how hard it is to trust the people around you when you're the don. Franco is entirely trustworthy and I'm grateful for it in every way.

"Come on," I say to Justine. "Time to get this taken care of."

"Don't sound so excited," Justine says with a little grimace.

I laugh lightly. "Sorry. I'm just...focused on what comes next."

"Your wedding should be special," my friend says sadly to me. "You shouldn't have to feel like you're just going through the motions."

"Maybe someday we can renew our vows at some kind of beautiful beachy location or something," I say with a shrug. "You know me, J. I'm not a romantic, not really. I care about trust and I can trust Angelo. That's enough for me for now."

We make our way out into the living room and I see that Angelo has his back to us. He's talking to the Catholic priest he has gotten to marry us. Franco, however, is looking right at us and his eyes widen with appreciation as he takes in Justine in the beautiful silky blue dress she put on.

He clears his throat and Angelo notices the sound. He turns, and his eyes land on me. His light green eyes widen in surprise and a sudden flare of heat makes my core clench with sharp desire.

The designer suit he is wearing flows over his lean, muscular frame perfectly, and his glasses make him look like some kind of computer genius or NASA engineer rather than a mafia boss. He looks good enough to eat, and my eyes travel hungrily from his long, strong legs to his broad shoulders, finally locking onto his green eyes that are filled with heat.

The priest moves to greet me, taking my hands in his slightly cold, dry fingers. "I knew your father well," he says to me. "I christened you, as a matter of fact." He steps back and looks at me without releasing my hands. I swear that I see tears in his eyes. "Your father would be so proud of how beautiful and strong you have grown up to be."

I'm not religious at all, never went to church as a kid, but I appreciate the affection I can feel coming from the priest. I realize how many other people missed out on my childhood who might otherwise have been able to bear witness to it. This man is just one of the many people who still remember me fondly and who never got to see me grow up.

I ponder this, thinking of the tiny life nestled within me. Will he or she get the chance to stay in one place, to grow up safely? Will they get to know this man when they are christened? Will they play with Franco, ride bikes with Angelo, learn to bake with me?

It's hard to imagine a normal childhood. I hope that I'm capable of being a good mother to this child.

"It's lovely to meet you," I say to the old man holding my hands. I glance over at Angelo, who is still staring at me, rooted in place by the windows.

"Come, *bella*," the priest says to me, leading me toward Angelo. "Let's get you two kids married."

"Oh, one moment!" Franco says abruptly, hurrying from the room.

I look at Justine, who shrugs. She's not in the loop about whatever he has planned either, apparently.

Franco shows back up a moment later with a bouquet for each of us. To my surprise, my eyes fill with tears at the thoughtful gesture. I take the flowers and breathe deeply of their scent.

"Thank you," I manage to say around the tightness in my throat.

"You can't get married without flowers," Franco says. "Or at least, that's what my mother always said." He clears his throat again, looking a little uncomfortable at having revealed so much about himself. Justine tucks herself in next to him, looping her arm through his.

"You look gorgeous, *Tesoro mio,*" Angelo says to me as I join him by the huge windows on the other side of the room.

"So do you," I say, then I laugh.

He smiles at me. "I'm glad to see you smiling."

"Shall we begin?" the priest asks.

I look at Angelo, and nod. He tilts his head to the priest and the man begins reading the words of the wedding ceremony to us.

The sound of his voice washes over me, my mind busy with questions about the future, my fingers tingling at Angelo's touch. The past month has been a whirlwind. I barely know how to feel about any of it.

But something about all of this has felt right, from the first moment that I saw Angelo standing by my mother's grave in his black suit and those glasses. From the first moment that I met his glade-green gaze, I knew that I belonged with him. Getting married just feels natural, inevitable, and right.

I realize I'm supposed to be repeating my part of the vows, and I quickly say my part, looking at Angelo steadily.

He holds his hand out to Franco, who passes him a ring. I realize with a jolt that it's a different ring. It's not the same ring I have been wearing for a couple of weeks since we publicly announced our engagement at the meeting with Guiseppe and the other men.

"How…?" I start to ask.

Angelo looks over at Justine with a smile.

I grin at my friend. "Oh…I see," I say. Bless Justine for knowing me so well. The ring is beautiful and exactly what I would have chosen for myself. It makes this all feel so much more like the real thing. I'm grateful to her and to Angelo for knowing that she could help make this part of the ceremony much more special for me.

"You may kiss the bride," the priest says to us.

I look up at Angelo through my lashes, suddenly shy. Always before we have kissed in the cover of darkness, or in the wildness of emotion after something dangerous has happened. There have been few interactions between us that anyone would think of as normal. I realize that I don't quite know how to kiss Angelo in front of other people like it's the most natural thing in the world.

He seems to be feeling the same reservations, or maybe he's just reacting to my own shyness. He reaches out and lifts my chin with his finger, smiling crookedly at me as he looks down at me from his greater height. He looks very young in this moment, his eyes sparkling behind his glasses and his well-cut mouth begging to be kissed.

"Shall we?" he asks me teasingly, bringing his mouth close to mine.

I look at his lips as they get closer, then close my eyes, surrendering to him, to this moment. His lips are soft at first, just barely touching mine, but then they move more insistently, and suddenly, he's the Angelo that I know, the Angelo who plunders my body in a fit of emotion, hurting and pleasing me in equal measure.

I kiss him back for a moment, already wet for him, feeling my heart racing in my chest. There's a small cough beside us and we jump apart abruptly as though we have been caught doing something wildly inappropriate, which maybe is what we were doing after all.

The priest winks at us, then walks away, gesturing to Franco. He takes Justine's hand to his lips, pressing a kiss to the back of it, before getting into the elevator with the priest to take him back home.

"That was hot," Justine says to us in her best Paris Hilton imitation. It's an old joke between us and I dissolve into immediate giggles.

Angelo shakes his head a little. "Come along, you two. Let's have some champagne to celebrate."

"Do you feel married?" Justine asks me as we wander into the kitchen.

I step out of my shoes and just leave them in the middle of the marble floor. I pad into the kitchen, which is spotless again, but my mind keeps seeing the red of Gianni's blood spreading over the white counter, spilling onto the starkly white floor. I blink a little to remove the vision from before my eyes and manage a smile.

"I don't know," I admit. "Everything has been moving so fast."

"You just need the wedding night to make it real," Justine says with certainty, nodding to herself as she pounds the first glass of champagne she was poured. "More please," she says, offering up her glass to Angelo again.

He lifts a brow at her, but fills her glass again. "Mind that you don't get in too much of a hurry," he says to her. "That stuff isn't cheap."

She laughs and waves a hand. "I know, sorry. It's just, being in here..." she gestures around the kitchen with a moue of distaste.

I nod, since I myself have been struggling to spend any time in the kitchen at all since last night.

"Let's go sit in here," Angelo says, grabbing the bottle and leading the way over to the formal living room. He turns on the gas fireplace and settles into one of the leather chairs near it. He grabs my wrist as I get closer to him and tugs me into his lap. I spill into it in a swath of heavy lace, giving a little squeak as I land.

I wriggle a little and grin. He's already hard for me.

Justine eyes us speculatively, but just sips at her drink. She turns to look at the fire, her beautiful profile lit with the orange glow.

"Is it ever safe?" she asks abruptly, pressing the glass to her lips as she stares into the flames. "I mean for people like you two. Is it ever *not* dangerous?"

Angelo sighs, rubbing a hand over my back. I resist the urge to purr like a cat at his touch.

"This is not normal, if that's what you're asking," he replies. "But it's never actually totally safe, I suppose. That's why we have guards, security and all the rest." He gestures around the room vaguely with his free hand.

"What about when you have kids?" she asks, and my heart squeezes in my chest. I know she won't tell Angelo our secret, not without permission, but this feels too close for comfort.

Angelo is silent for a moment, also looking at the flames. "I suppose I hadn't ever thought I would have children," he finally admits. "But if we do have children, we will do our best to keep them safe. Just like your parents did their best to keep you safe," he says to me.

I crane my head to look at his handsome face and I see the sincerity in his gaze. He means that, and I relax some. He might not know that we are going to be having a baby, but I can hear and see the sincerity in him now, talking about children we might have.

Justine nods. "That's all anyone can do, I guess."

"Do you want to go home now?" Angelo asks her without looking at her. He's still looking at me, drinking me in. The air between us changes, filling with sexual tension. I feel him lift his hips slightly, nudging his hard-on against me where it's disguised by the fall of my wedding dress.

Justine glances over at us, then smiles a little. "I haven't decided yet," she says, rising to her feet. "However, I know when I've worn out my welcome." She waggles her fingers at us before walking toward the elevator. She drops her glass off in the kitchen on the way by, then gets into the elevator and leaves us alone.

"So," Angelo says to me, adjusting my weight on his lap. "What shall we do with our evening?

I giggle and roll my eyes. "Oh, fuck off," I tell him. "You know I've been dying to have you rip this dress off me and fuck me senseless since the ceremony."

His laugh is loud and full, and it warms my heart to hear his joy. I have realized just how fleeting happiness can be in our world and I don't want to waste a drop of it.

"As ever, Sophia Agostini, your wish is my command."

Chapter Seventeen

Angelo

I feel drunk on her. She floods my senses, makes it hard to think about the family, our safety, the future, anything but the here and now. I am desperate to get her out of the heavy, silk dress, my fingers fumbling as I try to manage the tiny buttons that march down the back.

"Why do they make these things like this?" I mutter in annoyance, as I work my way down the row of buttons. My injured hand is not helping me at all. "This is ridiculous." My cock throbs with the same frustration that I'm feeling.

She laughs, the sound musical, carefree, as she cranes to look over her shoulder. She's holding her long, heavy hair out of the way so that I can struggle without also having to deal with her hair hanging down her back.

"I suspect it's tradition to torture the groom in as many ways as possible," she says with another giggle.

I grumble a little, but smile. "It's working," I say. I sigh with relief as I finally get the last button free.

"Phew!" she says, wriggling out of the heavy dress. I watch in appreciation as her lithe body wiggles in front of me, sending the dress to pool around her ankles. "That thing is heavy."

"You looked beautiful in it," I say honestly, reaching out to trail my fingers down her back. Her skin is soft and she smells amazing. I should find out what perfume she wears so I can be sure that she has plenty of it on hand.

"Thank you," she says, looking back at me again before turning and starting to take off all of her undergarments. "Justine did a great job pulling all of this together at the last moment."

"She's a wizard with planning these things," I agree, licking my lips as I watch her take off her bra. Her breasts, which are the perfect handful, bounce free of the garment. I immediately give in to temptation and cup them in my hands, rubbing my thumbs over her nipples. She stretches like a cat, pressing into my touch.

"Are you happy to be Mrs. Castiglia?" I ask her. I try not to let her know how much it means to me to have her be happy as my wife. We have never talked about our feelings with each other in any depth. There hasn't been time. I hate to contemplate finding out that she feels like this relationship is a prison.

She's silent for an extended period, just enjoying my fingers kneading her flesh. Suddenly, she gasps and pulls back, holding a hand over her breast. She looks strangely guilty as she glances up at me, and I frown.

"What's wrong?" I ask her, concerned.

She forces a smile onto her face again, and I wonder if maybe I imagined what I thought I had seen in her gaze before. "Oh, just a little tender. That happens sometimes." She steps out of the undergarments on the floor and leans her lithe form against me. "Sorry to interrupt the cadence of things."

I smile at her and press a kiss to her lips. "Your breasts feel extra delicious today. I like it," I murmur. I wrap my fingers into her hair and tug her head back, exposing her neck and showering it with nipping kisses.

She lets her head hang into my hands, and I press my lips to hers. The kiss starts out gentle but turns into something fierce, possessive and territorial. She gives as good as she's getting, nipping at my lower lip, pressing her body into mine and tugging against the restraint of my hand tangled in her hair, tugging her head back.

"You're still dressed," she says softly, pulling away from me. She looks up at me, her hazel eyes dark with passion.

"I undressed you. It's your turn," I tell her with a grin.

She smiles back, and I release her hair. She starts unbuttoning my dress shirt, then leans forward to press small kisses to the skin that is exposed as each button gives way. She helps me get out of my well-cut suit jacket, then pulls the shirt out of the waistband of my pants, shoving it down my arms.

She pauses with her long fingers on my belt, biting her lip and looking at me provocatively. My cock presses toward her unconsciously, and she smiles for real.

"Eager, are we?" she mutters, removing my belt and unzipping my slacks.

"Always," I say huskily. I have never felt this for a woman. I want to sink inside of her so badly that I'm shaking with need. It should be frightening to be this obsessed with her, but it's not. Wanting her, feels as natural as breathing to me by now and I can't imagine any other form of existence.

She slips my slacks down, then runs a finger under the elastic of my boxer briefs. She walks around me, her finger skimming against my heated flesh, just under the edge of my underwear. She pauses to give my ass an appreciative smack.

"Such a sexy bum," she says, a little bit of an English accent tinging her words.

"Glad you think so," I tell her. "I work hard to keep it like that. Also, you sound like an English girl when you say dirty things."

She laughs. "That all right with you?" she asks me, broadening the accent further as she circles around to my front.

"I love it," I tell her, looking at her from under lowered eyelids. I feel drunk with desire, loose in my joints, under her thrall.

"Bet you'll love this even more," she says saucily, the English accent still rounding out her words. She slips off my underwear and my cock springs out toward her eagerly. She smiles down at it appreciatively for a moment, before hunkering down in her tall heels, and taking it into her mouth.

I thrust forward into the warmth of her mouth immediately, closing my eyes and placing a hand on her head. Her hair is silky beneath my fingers as she sucks on me, her small hands wrapping around the remainder of my length. I don't know if she's incredibly good at this, or if it's the sight of her squatting in her high heels, her pussy on display as she sucks me off that is making it so hard for me to keep from busting immediately in her mouth.

"Jesus, that's good," I manage to say.

"He's not here," she says before sucking me into her mouth again. "It's just you and me," she adds, before going back to work.

I allow her to suck on me for a moment more, before I gently pull her head away. "Too much more of that, and this wedding night will be over before it began."

She smiles at me, and I glance down to see her pussy throb once. She rises athletically to her feet, standing before me in her sky-high heels, beautifully naked.

"I have never had to work so hard to keep myself in check," I tell her, stepping closer and reaching down to touch her. She's soaking wet, and she gives a little moan of want as I slip my fingers inside of her, teasing, then withdrawing. "You make me crazy."

"The feeling is mutual," she whispers, her eyes half-closed.

"Since we are taking turns in service to one another…" I say, before kneeling before her and sucking her clit into my mouth. She's soaking wet, and the taste of her is incredible.

She clenches my hair in her fingers, pressing against my mouth and tongue, moaning. I wrap my hand around her slim, muscular thigh, enjoying the contrast of strong muscles and soft, feminine skin. I delve my tongue inside of her, discovering the places that she likes the best, feeling the rising tremors that indicate she's spiraling toward orgasm.

Her legs start to tremble, and a trickle of moisture runs down her thigh. "Angelo…I don't think I…" she gasps out, before she starts to wobble in her high heels.

I rise immediately and tumble us backward onto the bed, her hair flying up to fall over her breasts in a silky cascade, tangling in my fingers and smelling of her perfume.

"Please, Angelo, please," she moans, writhing a little on the bed, lifting her hips toward me plaintively. "I'm so close."

I shake my head a little. "Trust me, *Tesoro mio,*" I say. I nudge her wetness with the head of my cock, but don't allow myself to slip inside. It's almost impossible not to ram into her with mindless abandon. It's all my body wants, but I hold back.

"Please," she mewls, arching off the bed, trying to force me to slip inside of her. "Please, I want you."

"I know you do," I reply, nudging my cock through her slickness again, letting just the head slip inside of her. I withdraw as soon as she tries to lift her hips to meet me. "Which is why you can't have me...yet."

"Angelo," she says, her tone growing a bit annoyed. She presses up toward me, and sheathes herself around me entirely with an excited cry.

"Fuck," I mutter, barely managing to force myself to pull out of her again. "Patience," I mutter to her as I lift myself off of her body a little.

I trail kisses down her neck, along her collarbone, and suck a nipple into my mouth. She arches into my mouth wildly, desperate for release, tossing her head on the bed. I continue on my way, ignoring my raging cock, kissing along her ribs, pressing my lips to her navel, then trailing my warm breath over the skin of her mound. She cants her hips up with a cry, her pre-orgasm shaking starting again.

"Oh, Angelo," she pleads. "I'm going to die if I don't come."

"Well, we can't have that," I say back. I draw closer to her again, allowing myself to come to rest against the wetness of her. The heat pouring from her hungry pussy makes my head spin, and my hips jerk in her direction before I can stop them. Hissing with annoyance at myself, I slow down, pressing a hand to her body just below her navel.

"Slow down, *Tesoro mio*," I whisper to her, moving slowly, so slowly within her, sheathing myself one fractional bit at a time. "Let me do the work. Let me pleasure you."

She draws in a deep breath, her languorous eyes meeting mine. She nods once, the movement almost imperceptible, before relaxing slightly into the bed. I continue pressing forward, my cock parting her heated flesh one tiny bit at a time. Her trembling increases as she catches her lower lip in her teeth, clearly struggling to hold still and let me fuck her this way.

I finally seat myself fully inside of her, and close my eyes as I will my cock to wait for just a moment, to extend the moment.

"Angelo, I swear to God if you don't..." she starts to say, her eyes flashing at me.

I silence her with a kiss, and press even further into her, nudging, pressing, stretching. She gasps loudly, her hands grasping the bedspread.

"Come with me, *Tesoro mio*," I tell her, feeling my orgasm poised to flood over me. I press forward yet again, feeling her internal trembling, feeling her thighs shaking where they are wrapped around my waist.

"Oh my God, Angelo!" she screams, coming violently, shaking and trembling, her wetness rushing over my cock and spilling across her thighs. I pump inside of her twice, and follow her over the edge, roaring with a pleasure that feels like it's tearing me apart from the inside out.

I just manage to keep myself from collapsing onto her, crushing her with my weight as I shake and snap with the jolts of ecstasy. I have never, ever experienced anything like this. I feel like I might die, but I would welcome death if it feels like this.

"Oh my lord," she whispers between noisy breaths. "Oh my God."

"Agreed," I say, my voice deep, hoarse, like I've been yelling at a concert or speaking loudly for hours.

I manage to tumble onto my side, tugging her with me so I can pull her into me. I stroke my hand slowly up and down her back, soothing us both, quieting the remaining aftershocks of the intense pleasure we just experienced.

"I will take this as a sign that you are okay with being Mrs. Castiglia," I say, dropping a kiss on her brow.

She chuckles. "How can I complain when you can do *that* to me?"

I laugh lightly. "I should be thanking you. For so many reasons."

She sighs a little and snuggles closer. "See that you don't forget it."

We are silent for a moment or two, and then I say, "I wish that we could go on a honeymoon. I'm sorry about the timing of all of this. I'm sure that this isn't what you imagined when you thought about your wedding day."

She leans away a little bit to look at me. "Well, to be fair, when I thought about my wedding day the last time, I was a little girl and I couldn't have imagined most of what this night would entail." She trails her fingers over my cock, which is still at half-mast. It twitches toward her despite this.

"Fair enough," I say with a smile. "Do you want a honeymoon?"

She shrugs. "It would be nice, eventually, I guess. But I know it's not possible right now."

I appreciate that she's so practical. She often amazes me with her determination to get things done. She is dogged, and tackles jobs with precision and energy, both big and small.

"I'm sure that there's something that we can do over the next couple of days," I press. I want her to be happy. I want her to feel appreciated.

She is quiet for a moment. Then she says, "Well, there is one thing I have been wishing I could do."

I draw back a little. "Name it."

She bites her lip, but she replies to my question. "Well...when I was a kid, my mom used to take me to the ice skating rink this time of year, and then we'd have hot chocolate or sweets from a food cart nearby. It was...we were...so happy." Her voice sounds thick with tears, and I felt a pang of sadness for her.

"We can do that," I tell her with a smile.

"Okay," she says easily. "When?"

I lift up onto my elbow. "How about right now?"

"Wait, what?"

I grin at her. Her idea sounds fun. I can't remember the last time I had any fun. "Sure," I say with a shrug. "We'll just bring some guards with us."

She sighs. "I don't really want to have to go if we have to have guards," I admit. "It still feels weird to be watched while I'm having fun. It's so...awkward."

I nod. I can understand that even though I'm very used to being followed everywhere I go. I think for a moment, looking at her, feeling the lingering pleasure from fucking her tingling through me. I would do anything for her, I realize. Because I love her.

Love. The realization makes me feel like someone hit me over the head. I stare at her as I realize just how long this has been the case. I have no idea if she feels the same way, but I want her to.

"Let's go without them, then," I tell her against my better judgment. "It's not far."

Her grin is dazzling and I feel like a hero seeing it. "Oh my gosh, yay!" she exclaims. She bolts off the bed, then looks down at herself in her tall, sexy heels, sticky with our pleasure. "Shower," she says, jogging toward the bathroom, her firm booty bouncing a little with each jogging step.

I chuckle, rising from the messy bed and stepping over our discarded clothing to join her in the bathroom. She's taking off her heels and dancing around excitedly, and I smile at her.

"Dress warm!" she sings out as she gathers her hair into a big, messy bun before stepping into the shower. "It's surprisingly chilly on the ice. Plus, if you fall, the extra layers are good for some protection."

"Can I join you?" I ask her with amusement.

"Oh," she laughs. "Yes, of course." She pushes open the shower door, then goes back to rinsing off.

I watch her for a moment, basking in her joy. I realize that she hasn't been this happy since I met her and I feel a ridiculous amount of pride in having generated this response in her. I know we shouldn't go out without a guard, but she is so excited about my proposed adventure, that I can't bear the thought of ruining it.

I think to myself that I will send Franco a text. Just to make sure that he's keeping tabs on our location via location sharing. I'm not a complete fool, even if my new wife is encouraging me to throw caution to the wind just this once.

I get out of the shower and towel off, then quickly send Franco a text.

I don't like this idea. I can come and hang out where she can't see me.

I sigh. I would feel better if he did that, but I don't want to break her trust, or ruin the happy mood that she's in.

I'll update you if anything strange seems to be going on. You can probably see us from your bedroom window.

"Something wrong?" Sophia asks, her voice tense.

"Nope. Hurry up! It's going to be dark soon."

Chapter Eighteen

Sophia

I practically skip as we cross the street, my fingers linked with Angelo's. I look up at the evening sky. It looks like snow, and I grin. I love snow.

"I love snow," I say aloud to Angelo as we walk toward the park. "It snows in the UK, but it's not the same. Mostly it's just gloomy and damp all the time. My apartment always had mold in the winter."

I shudder. There were many things I loved about my life in the UK, but the never-ending wetness wasn't one of them.

"I've only been there a few times," I tell her, allowing her to swing my arm a little as she skips along next to me. "But it seems nice. I like the pubs."

She chuckles. "Pubs are cool, I agree," she says with a nod. "I feel like they appeal more to tourists than locals, but they are fun to hang out in."

"When you did this in the past," I say to her, glancing over my shoulder to make sure I don't see anything suspicious going on, "did you go with your mother and your father?"

She nods. "Yeah. My dad was more involved when I was little. I'm not sure what changed."

Angelo pulls his phone of out his pocket and I can see that Franco has texted him before he tilts the phone away.

"Everything okay?" I ask. My voice sounds tense, even to my ears.

He shakes his head and pockets his phone. "No, sorry. Just answering some business texts."

I roll my eyes. "You don't even take any time off, do you?"

He looks at me askance as we approach the skating rink. "That makes you mad, doesn't it?"

I admire the twinkling lights and the festive air in this area of the park. It's just as magical as I remember it being.

"Not mad," I say slowly. "It just brings up bad memories. Before we...left...my mom and my dad were always busy with the business, the family, the emergencies. I didn't get to see them very much. That's why our nights in the park, or the rare times that we traveled for fun were so special to me."

"I'm sorry that your childhood was so...eventful," he says to me.

I laugh loudly. "That's one way to describe it," I say with a shake of my head. "Come on, let's get our skates."

I drag him toward the counter where he pays for our skate rental and a locker for our shoes. We get our skates on and I happily glide out onto the ice, the muscle memory from years past helping me to make slow, looping circles with ease.

"Come on!" I call as I twirl around a bit awkwardly.

"I'm working on it," he says to me. He steps up to the edge of the skating rink and hesitates. I turn sideways to stop myself and smile at him. He looks...uncertain, and it warms my heart.

"Come on, scaredy cat," I tease. "Get out here."

"If I break my neck, you are to blame," he says to me, wagging a finger in my direction.

I roll my eyes. "Yeah, yeah. Hurry up!"

I watch as he gingerly steps onto the ice, losing his balance a little bit, and sliding over to the wall.

"Here," I say. "Do it like this."

I start coaching him about how to slide across the ice, and he starts to get more confident and finds his balance. My cheeks are pink from the cold and the grin on my face practically hurts it's so wide. I didn't realize how much I had missed having fun like this. I feel lighter, happier, than I have felt in years.

"See? It's fun!" I exclaim, doing a little swirl and then skating away from him for a moment.

"Come out here and dance with me!" I call to him as I skate backward and forward in the middle of the rink.

"Ummm," he says hesitantly. He barely dodges some other skaters, apologizing as he stumbles his way out to me. "Easier said than done," he grumbles as he draws close to me.

"Sure," I say, taking his gloved hands and spinning us slowly around as I take the lead. "But worth it."

We skate in lazy circles, his balance growing more certain as he allows me to take the lead. I love this about him, that he lets me be in charge when it's only fair that I should be. I appreciate that he doesn't try to tell me what to do, or who to be. It's special, to be seen and treated like a complete human being. So few people in our lifestyle allow their wives or daughters to have any say in what happens to them.

"This was a good idea," he says to me, his voice low and intimate.

I look up at him, and find that he's gazing down at me with lust-hazed eyes. I lean a little closer and stretch up to kiss his lips. I already feel the hunger tugging at me, pulling in my belly despite the cold.

"Thank you for indulging me," I say back as I draw away. I can tell we aren't going to spend much more time skating. He clearly has other things on his mind and I'm not interested in arguing. Besides, we really shouldn't stay out without a guard for long. I know it's not safe, and I don't want something bad to happen to us just because I wanted to feel free for a moment.

"You know what would make this little 'honeymoon' complete?" I inquire, my head tilted to the side.

A little smile tucks into the corner of his full mouth. "Nope, but you're going to tell me, aren't you?"

I giggle. "Hot chocolate. To go." I lean up and kiss him again, this time with more intensity, offering a promise of what is to come when we get back to the penthouse.

"Your wish is my command," he says to me with a silly bow that almost makes him fall on his face on the ice. I help catch him with a laugh, and then pilot us toward the edge of the rink to collect our shoes and turn in our skates.

We get changed back into our shoes, and then wander through the park toward the collection of food vendors that have taken up residence not far from the skating rink. One of them offers a variety of hot chocolate, and we of course choose this food stand for our order.

"Mm, spicy," I say with my eyes closed, taking the first sip of my spicy cinnamon hot chocolate.

He sticks out his tongue. "Ick. I can't believe anyone likes cinnamon."

I shake my head at him deploringly. "You yanks and your horrible tastebuds," I say in my best, posh British accent.

He smiles at me. "Hey, you guys eat all kinds of boiled potatoes and stuff. Gross."

I giggle in reply, then pass him my hot chocolate. "I need to pee," I tell him apologetically. I feel like this must be part of my early pregnancy woes. When I'm not barfing my guts out, I'm peeing a hundred times a day.

He frowns a little. "I'll come over there with you. I don't want you to walk all by yourself through the park."

I sigh and put my hands on my hips. "The public restrooms are just over there," I say, pointing to the small building that's just beyond the food trucks. "Don't baby me. I'll be right back."

I turn, my scarf flying, and hurry toward the bathroom. It isn't very far away, and I also really don't want to pee myself in the middle of the park.

I hustle into the relative warmth of the bathroom and pee, then wash my hands with the freezing water coming out of the tap. I go to push back through the door I used to come in, but realize that it only opens one way. Rolling my eyes, I walk to the other end of the building and push open the "out" door. I step around the door and start to head back around the building, when a hand clamps down over my mouth.

I instantly start struggling, trying to make noise, trying to get free. This was a mistake, I see that now. I should never have convinced Angelo to come out here into the park without the guards. I was a fool.

I bite at the hand holding my face, but the person who grabbed me is wearing gloves. They are also quite large, and I am finding that I can barely move in their grip, let alone get any effective blows in that might free me.

"Stop struggling, little dove," a voice hisses in my ear, and I freeze.

Little dove. My father called me that. No one but my mother knows that this was what he always called me…except for…my heart turns to ice in my chest. Guiseppe.

I feel a hardness pressed against my side and I realize that he probably has a gun in his pocket. Resentment twists in my gut. He's like some kind of fictional mobster. He makes sure to use all the moves that you'd see in something like *Peaky Blinders*. But apparently, those moves work, if my current situation is any indication.

"Don't fight me," he hisses in my ear. "I don't actually give a shit about you, or your claim to your father's power. I want to kill Angelo, and you will lead him right to me. You're the perfect bait, little dove. How stupid of you to think that I don't have my men following you both at all times."

I want to say so much to him. Poisonous thoughts tumble through my brain and I wish that I could scald him with the violence of my anger like a hot kettle on bare skin. To think that this man watched me grow up, was my father's right-hand man, and yet doesn't care about my existence at all.

He starts rummaging through my pockets, and finds my phone. He drags it awkwardly out of my pocket with one hand and I hear the screen smash as he stomps on it. I want to cry with frustration. Angelo and I had talked about getting bracelets that looked like real jewelry but had tracking devices in them. I had reluctantly agreed to wear one, but he hadn't pressed me on the topic. Now I felt like a damn fool for not immediately putting one on.

"We are going to back away from here now, so that lover boy doesn't see us leaving." He tugs on me, forcing me to back up. I start to struggle again, and he grips my face more tightly, causing me to squeak in pain. I taste blood on my tongue.

"I hear congratulations are on order," Guiseppe says to me, his lips touching my ear. I shudder with revulsion. "Married so quickly. It must be true love."

I try to throw my elbow back into him, but he pinches my face so hard that my eyes water.

"Remember that I don't care what condition you are in while you are in my care, dove. I won't kill you, but I don't have to make your stay with me comfortable."

I feel a twinge of nausea and I suddenly remember that I'm not alone anymore. My heart clenches in my chest. *The baby*. I relax in his grip, allowing him to drag me through the tree-lined park planters toward the street. My moment for a surprise escape is long over, and anything that I do now to thwart him could hurt the baby.

Angelo! I think, wishing that I could connect with him telepathically. *Please come looking for me. Please come to see if I'm okay.*

I strain my eyes to see if he has come toward the bathrooms, but it's getting hard to see the little building through the vegetation all around us. I finally lose sight of the bathroom structure and my heart sinks.

Guiseppe hustles me into a black SUV and the driver immediately takes off. He pulls the gun from his pocket and points it at me.

"Don't try anything foolish," he orders me. "Not if you want to get out of this in one piece. You will see that I can be merciful. I have a plan that will allow you both to be together…so long as you meet my demands. It would be a shame for you to be disfigured because you fought against my good will so hard."

I look at him with disgust. He's still handsome, in a dissipated way. I remember a couple of the other girls that I grew up with thought he was dreamy and it makes me feel sick. There's something utterly terrible about the face of evil being beautiful. I'm glad that he's starting to age enough to make his outward appearance a fair warning for his inner ugliness.

I try to keep track of where we are going, but suddenly, someone leans over the backseat and yanks a sack over my head. It smells strongly of cologne and I gag immediately. My stomach roils with pregnancy nausea and I try not to breathe through my nose.

Pay attention to sounds and feel the turns of the car, my mother and father had told me when I was little. At the time, I had thought that they were being worrywarts. Who would kidnap me with our large security details, bulletproof vehicles, and fenced compounds? Now, however, I was grateful for the advice that they had drilled into me during my childhood. It was coming in handy now as I tried to ignore my raging nausea and pay attention to where we were going.

I thought that we might be heading toward the port. The direction of each turn was correct and despite the heavy cologne smell from the bag over my head, I caught a strong whiff of fishy sewage at one point when someone in the car rolled down the window to throw out a cigarette.

I tried to remember where Guiseppe's holdings were at the port, then my blood ran cold in my veins. What if he was going to put me on a ship? What if he was going to take me somewhere else? I knew that Angelo was exploring rumors that Guiseppe was involved in human trafficking. If that were true, he could send me anywhere and I wouldn't be able to escape.

I fight against my panic, willing myself not to freak out yet. Angelo would probably have noticed I had vanished by now. He couldn't be far away.

I will keep you safe, little one, I think to the tiny life nestled inside my body. I feel tears prickle at the corners of my eyes. I needed to think of both of us and I needed to make a plan as quickly as possible.

Chapter Nineteen

Angelo

Where was she?

I lean to the side, sipping at my spiked drink. The alcohol is taking the edge off the ache in my hand, which is nice. I can't wait for it to be back to normal. It's a small injury, but so inconvenient in so many ways.

Surely, it shouldn't take this long to pee. But girls were always taking forever to do everything, so I rock back and forth on my heels for a bit longer, my eyes trained on the dingy bathroom structure.

Finally, I decide that I need to go see what is up. Maybe she isn't feeling well. I remember that Justine had said she had had the flu or something last week. Maybe she was lightheaded and was leaning against the wall of the building.

I wander toward the bathroom and realize that the door in is not also set up as an exit, so I go toward the back of the building. Maybe I can just pull the door and call to her from there.

As I walk around the back of the building, my heart leaps into my chest at the sight of a smashed iPhone on the ground. It's sparkly and gold, just like Sophia's.

I hurry over, dropping the drinks without caring that they have spilled all over the ground.

The phone is dead when I pick it up, but I would know the case anywhere. Justine had brought it with her from the UK and they had both been giggling over it. It was a designer brand or something.

I text Franco, *9-1-1. Sophia is in danger. Get down here to park and meet me.*

I hurried around the area, trying to find other clues or signs of where she had gone. My blood felt like ice in my veins as I realized that there was nothing, no sign of where she had gone or who had taken her. However, I had a good idea.

"Dammit!" I curse. We had been so foolish. Why had I given in to her silly desire to have fun like normal people, without our guards accompanying us? An hour of fun was never worth this kind of risk and I felt like an asshole for allowing this.

On my way, Franco sends back. *The guards will get there first.*

I hurried back to the center of the park, scanning the area for my guards or for Guiseppe and his men.

There was no one else who could have taken her like this. No one else would have risked such a public kidnapping. And, I had to admit to myself, no one else could have stolen her from under my nose like this.

"Boss!"

I turned to see a small group of my guards running toward me. I fill them in quickly and tell them to spread out and look for any clues at all, her scarf, signs of a scuffle, cars that are parked on the street that look suspicious, anything.

I watch them all disperse and look around with frustration.

I thought of the damn tracker jewelry that I had bought for us. She had been so upset by the idea of wearing it, that I hadn't pressed her about it. Now that seemed like just one of many stupid choices we had both made over the past few weeks.

My eyes landed on the little group of vendors where we had gotten our hot chocolate. I strode over, immediately demanding if anyone at the hot dog stand had seen my wife or where she had gone. I went from cart to cart, but no one had seen anything.

"Fuck!" I growl, kicking at a rock near the edge of one of the planters. It hurt my foot and I grimace. Childish behavior wasn't going to get me anywhere. I tell myself to calm down.

"Excuse me."

I glance over my shoulder to see a nervous-looking young man looking at me. He was glancing around like he thought he might be in danger and I could practically see him quivering.

"Yes?" I try not to be short with him. Maybe he had something useful to tell me.

"Well, you seem like you might be looking for someone...or something," he stammers. "Is it your...girlfriend that you skated with?"

I nod. "My wife, yes." I describe her briefly to the young man, and he nods.

He swallows hard, "I think I saw her being pushed into a big, black car over there by the dumpsters. I was taking out the trash from the skating rink. A man...he looked like mafia...like you...he was dragging her, and then he pushed her into the car and they drove off." He gulps again and gives me an apologetic look.

I nod. "That's helpful. Where did the car go?"

"That way," the man says, pointing in the direction of the docks. I saw them take the first left at the corner of the park, and then another right."

"Thank you," I say to him. "What's your name?"

He shakes his head. "It's okay. No need to do anything for me," he says as he hurries off.

I sigh. Everyone in this city knew a mob man when they saw one. I didn't blame him. It was brave of him to stick his neck out at all.

They went to the docks based on what a witness said, I texted Franco and my guards.

I'll pick you guys up, Franco sent back. He dropped a pin in the chat, and I moved toward it.

The docks. We had just blown up the shipment of illegal goods that Guiseppe had stashed there, but I didn't think he would take her to a place that we were already familiar with.

I can't help but ponder the rumors that I had been looking into about his interest in human trafficking.

I didn't know a lot about the business since it is entirely despicable, but I know that most of the men who participated in it own ships that are used for other purposes. The women and children were typically smuggled inside metal shipping containers that are labeled as innocuous goods.

I pull out my phone. I need to call in a favor. I look at the contact in my phone and grimace.

I hate bringing Rudolpho Masi into this. He left years ago, made a clean break. But I need the help of a skilled hacker and he is the best person to reach out to for this kind of need.

I hesitate, thinking of the day that I had handed him his forged documents.

Rudolpho was a small, slender man, entirely ordinary, but his dark eyes blazed with intensity in his narrow face. If you never met his gaze, you would have no idea who you were dealing with. He has the perfect cover in his ordinariness. Only his eyes ruin his disguise.

He had wanted to go to a place with a beach to surf, sip on fruity drinks and stay away from trouble. The FBI had wanted to hire him, but he had an everlasting hatred of cops and couldn't bring himself to hack for them.

I helped him escape. I was proud of that. I hated the idea of bringing him into this.

"Nothing else to do," I mutter to myself, making the decision to do it.

I hit the call button as I strode toward the pin that Franco had sent. The line is ringing as I climb into the car. I was afraid that Rudolpho wouldn't pick up, but then I heard his tight, staccato voice on the other end of the line.

"Long time no chat, Angelo."

I let out a sigh. "I need a favor, Rudy."

"I thought so," Rudy answers sagely.

"It's Sophia. Guiseppe has her."

There was a silence on the end of the line. Rudy had grown up as part of Sophia's father's house. He would have been one of the children who played with her when she was small.

"She's back?" he asks, his voice tighter than usual.

"We're married. We honored the betrothal. Guiseppe is not happy."

"Clearly," he says drily. "Fine. What do you need?"

"I need to know if Guiseppe or any of his buddies owns a shipping company, or has a ship that they might be using for human trafficking. I think he might try and take her out of the country to force my hand. He wants to take over the Agostini family and he's crazy enough to do anything to accomplish his goal."

"I got out," Rudy reminds me.

I blow out a breath. "I know. You can say no. I would understand."

"Fuck," Rudy says quietly. "That's the thing about you, Angelo. You're so fucking nice that it's hard to say no to you."

I grin to myself as we drive toward the docks.

"I'll check it out. Dig up anything that I can," Rudy tells me. "I'll book a plane ticket too. You need someone like me and I know you don't have anyone."

"Don't do anything crazy on our behalf," I urge him, worry lancing through me. Rudy was a good dude. He didn't need to come back to the life for me or for Sophia. I was already asking too much of him by calling in a favor.

"I'm goddamn bored," he drawls in my ear. "You can take the life out of the mobster, but you can't take the mobster out of the mob...or something like that. Plus, Sophia is a good person. I'll be in touch."

"Thanks, Rudy," I say to him just before he hung up. Calls with Rudy were always brief so that no one could trace the call. I was used to him hanging up without saying goodbye.

"Rudy doing some digging?" Franco says sagely.

I nod. "Good guy."

"The best," Franco echoes, navigating another turn.

I only hope his help won't be too little, too late.

Chapter Twenty

SOPHIA

Everything hurts.

They have been torturing me for hours, asking for access codes, safe codes, the information about various businesses. I don't know any of the information that they want. I haven't had time to do anything other than marry Angelo and best Guiseppe at a duel.

It's ironic that I don't have the answers they sought. I would have given them up. I didn't give a flying fuck about my father's legacy or our family holdings. I would give them all up just to keep the baby in my belly safe and to get them to leave me alone.

I struggle backward to lean against the wall. One of my eyes is swollen shut, and my lip is painfully split. I winced as I breathed. Guiseppe had kicked me in the ribs in a rage when I didn't even know the gate code to the family estate outside the city. I thought I had a few broken ribs.

Did he think he was going to set himself up at the compound and lord it over everyone from there? He truly was mad. He didn't need the gate code for the compound anyhow. He could have just gone there and snapped his fingers and gotten inside.

I wasn't sure if he remembered the good old days with my father in charge differently, or if he just didn't want to admit that he was beating me for the fun of it at this point. He was *so angry* that I had bested him and so hurt that no one around him but his few friends seemed to think that he was don material.

I manage an internal smile as I think about the late, great Guiseppe Costa angrily beating a woman because she's better at being a man than he is. How my father would have laughed at his rage.

I feel an unexpected quiver of sadness wash over me at the thought of my father. I had made sure never to think of him for most of my childhood and then I had almost forgotten about him as I got older. It feels strange to be so sure of what he would have wanted, what he would have thought, now that I was walking in his shoes.

I wasn't sure if my mother would have been happy that I was so comfortable in the role of female don, but it couldn't be helped. There was no one left to save us all from Guiseppe. I had to do what my father had not been able to do.

I knew that I was at the docks. I also knew that I was on a ship that was docked there. I could smell all kinds of human smells, all unpleasant, and I had a sneaking suspicion that this was the ship that Guiseppe and his people used to traffic people back and forth from other countries.

I wondered where I was going to be taken to. Russia? South America? Just another port of call in another state?

I didn't know much about human trafficking. Normally, I would have said thank God to that, but right now, it was an issue for me. I had a large blind spot for the situation I was in and it was making me nervous. I knew that Angelo would have the same blind spot.

My stomach turns over as the fishy smell of the harbor washes over me through the tiny crack in the window well above me. I try to resist, but can't. I lean over and wretch, my stomach long empty.

I thought I had a concussion to add to my morning sickness and I knew that my dehydration wasn't helping my cause either. I press an aching hand to my belly. One of my fingers is angled the wrong direction. For a while, they had held my hand down while someone slammed a hammer on the table near my fingers. Occasionally, they had let the hammer smash a finger.

Guiseppe had been cackling and telling me all about how I should be tough enough to handle this because I was a don now. Between the ridiculous stories about his glory days and his enjoyment of my torture, I had come to hate him with an entirely new passion.

He was a disgusting person. My father should have known better.

I slip in and out of unconsciousness now that my head has been injured and I feel a wave of sleepiness pass over me. My mind starts drifting, remembering.

"I don't like Uncle Guiseppe." My small voice was tremulous, indignant as I looked at my father.

"Why not, little dove?" my father asked in his deep, velvety voice. He had tweaked my nose in an effort to charm me out of my petulance.

"He gives me the creepy crawlies," I insisted, stamping my foot.

My father had laughed and picked me up. I stroked a hand over his shiny, dark hair. His eyes were so dark brown that they looked black as he regarded me with love.

"I have to have bad men working for me, little dove," he told me. "I need their help to do the scary things other men won't do."

"I don't want to marry a man like Uncle Guiseppe," I insisted.

My father smiled at me. "You won't, my dove. I have arranged a perfect match for you. A friend's boy. He's kind and loves animals. You will have lots in common."

"Does he have a pony?" I asked, my annoyance forgotten.

"Lots of them," my father had assured me. "You can ride together when you are old enough to meet."

"Okay, I guess," I had replied with a little shrug. "But boys are icky."

My father had laughed loudly at this. "You won't always think so, my dove."

The sound of footsteps jolts me awake. Where had that memory come from? I wonder if it was an actual memory, or just a fantasy my mind conjured up.

I feel a tear slip down my cheek and I dash it away angrily. This is no time for weakness. I need to figure out how to get out of here.

I thought of my father's handsome face and his strong arms. *I could use a little inspiration, papa,* I think to myself.

The steps are getting closer and I huddle in on myself. I have to protect the baby at all costs. I cannot let them hit me in the stomach or throw me around. It's my one, overarching goal at this moment. It's all I can control.

"Well, don't you look terrible," Guiseppe says in a happy tone of voice as he steps into the room. He spits in my direction and says something very rude in Italian.

"Your stupid husband has not found you, yet. How does that make you feel? Do you think less of him? Maybe you could have done better if the roles were reversed. After all, you are your father's daughter, even if it pains me to admit it."

He leans down and grabs my cheeks, pinching hard and bashing my head against the metal wall behind me.

I stifle my shriek of pain as I see stars. A flare of impotent rage floods through me, but I just huddle more tightly into a ball on the floor.

"Why do you hate him so much?" I grind out through the pain that clenches my jaw shut. I honestly don't understand what his problem with Angelo is. I would have thought he would be more focused on hating me than my husband.

Guiseppe looks at me like I'm simple. "I suppose you don't know the truth. After all, your mother hid you away so long ago. It was smart of her. She was a cunning bitch, that one. Your father knew where you were, but he made sure that none of the rest of us could get to you."

I feel a jolt of shock at his words. It had never occurred to me that my father would have made sure that we were protected all those years that we were living in the UK. I felt so, so stupid that I had thought that my mother and I had just been able to get away and start over.

It makes me realize that Angleo was right. My father had loved me and tried to protect me despite what my mother had done. Maybe he understood all too well why she had run.

"I can tell you the story, since you are a fool and never realized your true situation," Guiseppe says. "Really, you should have stayed in England. You were safer there than you ever will be here. Your father and Angelo's father saw to that."

That was a new wrinkle. Angelo's father had also helped to keep me safe? Why?

"You want to know why I am so angry at Angelo? You want to know why I want to kill him? Well, I will tell you a little story about Arnoldo Castiglia. He would have been your father-in-law, you see. He's been dead some time now, but that's no loss." He bares his teeth and then spits on the floor again near me. I eye the spittle with revulsion.

"Your father and Angelo's father were purists, you see. They believed that the Cosa Nostra could only be strong if full-blooded Sicilians were in charge. They looked down on the rest of us as less-than, all because we were only Italian, or perhaps even worse half-Italian."

He wanders around the room, his hands behind his back, lost in his memories.

"Your father and mother struggled to have children. You almost killed her and then she wasn't able to have any more kids. You would have to be the heir to the family, which, as you know, just isn't how things are done. So those two old men, they got together and made a plan. They betrothed you, just like medieval princes, to Angelo."

I didn't know my mother couldn't have children after she had me. It certainly never came up since she had avoided men like the plague after our escape. She had been chaste as a nun for all I knew for practically my entire life.

"The trouble with Angelo being considered the natural heir to the venerated Castiglia name, is that Arnoldo had another son, an older son, who should have been the rightful heir to his family."

I squint up at him despite the way that the room spins dizzily around me. What is he talking about?

Guiseppe laughs, a crazy laugh, that frightens me. All the hairs lift on the nape of my neck. "The trouble was, that son was impure, a half-blood, not good enough. Turns out that it is the fault of the child that their father chose to sleep with a maid from Mexico and get her pregnant. To hide the embarrassment of his great mistake, Arnoldo put his half-blooded son into the keeping of a man he could trust to hide his dirty little secret. Your father."

My brain feels sluggish, but I'm finally catching up. Suddenly, I realize what he means. My eyes pop open and I stare at him as comprehension washes over me like a wave.

"You," I say quietly, my voice choked.

He nods, the spark of insanity alive in his eyes. "Me. The half-blood, the shameful embarrassment to Arnoldo Castiglia. I was replaced by his full-blooded Sicilian son as soon as possible and was told to never hope to take my rightful place as the heir."

He paces some more, rage radiating off of him. I shrink back against the wall, scared to death of him. It's like being caged with a dangerous wild animal.

"So you see why I expected to take over for your father when he died. After all, you were a woman," he spat on the floor again, "and you ran away. You were not fit to be don. I didn't know about the betrothal, of course. I figured I would just take over and then I would fight Angelo to the death if necessary. After all, he had stolen my birthright. I deserved to take it back."

I watch him cautiously, not sure what to expect from him. I knew enough about mob politics to understand what he had been thinking. When great houses didn't have male heirs, often there was a contest of wills among the men who had served the family and the right-hand man tended to end up on top. But my father had realized what Guiseppe was, knew what kind of threat he was and so he had caged him in quite effectively.

I felt a new appreciation for my father's plan, alongside a new terror as I realized what the baby I was carrying would mean to Guiseppe. Angelo's and my child would be able to rightfully take over both of our houses, inheriting a shared legacy that would make them incredibly powerful.

Guiseppe stops pacing and stands next to me, looking up at the ceiling. He sighs and stretches out his arms over his head as if he is welcoming benediction from the beyond.

"Fuck you, father!" he screams out, the shout ringing through the tiny space. "And fuck you as well, Carlo!"

He turns toward me, his stare filled with hate. Like a snake, he shoots his hand out and grabs a hold of my hair, ripping me off the floor. I scream in pain as my ribs protest and my hair feels like it will be torn out at the roots.

He slams me onto the table in the center of the room and slaps me. I taste blood in my mouth, but I refuse to look at him.

"Look at me, you spoiled bitch!" he screams in my face. His spittle covers my face. "Look at me!" he shouts again, delivering another stinging slap to my cheek.

Resentfully, I open my good eye to glare at him. Rage floods through me. I think of sticking my thumbs in his eye sockets and prying his eyes out like grapes. I'm shaking with fury despite my bruises and broken bones.

"Ah, there is the proud Agostini blood singing to life in your useless little body. If only you had been a man." He sneers at me. "But then again, if you were a man, you would not be able to do the magic of women."

He grins at me like a jackal and pulls out a large switchblade. He flips it open and raises it over my exposed midsection like some kind of crazed priest.

"No!" I scream, trying to roll up in a ball to protect my womb. "Fuck you, Guiseppe!"

We grapple, and I feel the sudden cold sting of pain that indicates that he has cut the skin on my back with the blade. He's spitting curses at me, grappling with me painfully, but my fear has made me strong. I punch him in the face, screaming as my broken finger connects with his cheekbone. I will not let him kill my baby.

"You evil creature, Satan's spawn!" Guiseppe hisses as he struggles with me. He slips into Italian, most of which I don't understand, which is fine by me. I manage to roll off the table, getting free of his weight. I make a lunge for the door, but he's faster.

He grabs my shoulder and then wraps his hands around my throat. I struggle, trying to get free.

"Stop struggling right now, or I will give in to what I want most, and stab you in the belly," he spits at me.

I realize that he still holds the knife, and I freeze. I lock eyes with him, realizing that I'm crying, but also so angry that I feel sick.

"Your husband will be given a time to meet with me," Guiseppe says. "If he is wise, he will agree. He will give your father's legacy to me and I will probably allow this devil child to live."

He jabs the knife forward and I arch backward with a cry. I feel the tip of the knife skate across the surface of my skin, drawing blood.

"But so help me, if either of you double-crosses me, I will come back here and make Jack the Ripper look like an amateur."

He spits in my face and chucks me onto the floor in a heap. I lie gasping on the rusty metal surface, listening to him leaving. He slams the door behind him and locks it.

Groaning, I roll over onto my side, wrapping my arms around my belly. I barely even feel all my other injuries anymore. I must be going into shock.

"Just give him what he wants," I murmur to myself, wishing I could talk to Angelo. "I don't care what you give him so long as he stops hurting me."

I think of everything that Guiseppe told me. I have a whole new understanding of everything, really. If I make it out of here alive, there are things that I will change, things that Angelo and I can do better.

But I have to survive first.

Chapter Twenty-One

Angelo

"Here's what Rudy dug up," I tell Franco as I pull up the information that he had sent via encrypted email to me.

"Can we use it?" Franco asks.

I nod. "God, the man is so good at this. I'm not sorry he's said he's coming back," I admit as I pore over the pages and pages of intel that Rudy had been able to send in just an hour.

"There's a ship," I say eagerly as I skim the documents. "It's docked here. It's called *Il Fantasma*. Rudy says it belongs to a shell corporation that is actually Guiseppe's. He thinks that's where he might have taken Sophia."

Franco pulls a face. "Such an obvious name. What a disgusting bastard."

I nod. "There's something wrong with him," I agree. I had no idea why Sophia's father had kept him as his right-hand man. It had never made sense to me. Maybe he had been blind to his evil.

I get a text, and I frown. I don't recognize the number.

I open the text and see that it contains a pinned set of coordinates and a simple message.

Meet me. Give me what I want, or the bitch and the baby die.

"Baby?" I say to myself, my heart practically stopping in my chest. A baby. Oh my God. How did Guiseppe find out when she hadn't even told me yet? I thought of Justine saying that Sophia had had the flu last week. It wasn't the flu. It must have been morning sickness.

"Baby?" Franco echoes, but he doesn't sound surprised.

I glance over at him sharply. "You knew too?" I demand, feeling angry. "Did everyone but me know?"

Franco has the good grace to look sheepish. "Justine..." he says, then trails off.

I roll my eyes. "We really need to teach that girl to keep secrets better if she's going to be warming your bed all the time."

Franco chuckles softly, then sobers. "Okay, so what's the plan? We can't give him what he wants, but he clearly is crazy enough to kill Sophia."

"I feel like I'm missing something," I say, poring over the notes that Rudy sent me. Something isn't adding up for me. Why would Guiseppe be so willing to hurt Sophia just to get at me? I had thought he wanted to take over the Agostini family. If he hurt Sophia, many of the men would turn against him, making it hard for him to claim the don position uncontested. Unless that wasn't really what he wanted at all.

I remembered seeing something in Rudy's notes about a birth certificate or something. I scroll through the document until I find it again. An image of the birth certificate is attached. I make it bigger and then suck in a breath.

"What?" Franco asks me, leaning over to try and see what I'm looking at.

I turn wide eyes on him. Suddenly, it all makes sense. "Look at this," I say, thrusting my phone at Franco. "It's Guiseppe's birth certificate. Look at who is listed as his father."

Franco squints at the image, and then his mouth falls open. "Oh my God," he whispers.

I nod, taking my phone back. "It's all making sense now," I say, my mind already formulating a plan.

"It looks like the coordinates of the place he wants to meet are near the ship. I imagine he will want to put a bag over my head or something to make sure I can't tell where we are going."

Franco nods. "It's what we would do."

"My thinking is that you and the men can head to the ship while I'm meeting with Guiseppe. That way, you can have the element of surprise when it's just his men and no one else. Once you control the ship, you can ambush him when we arrive."

"I don't like you going to meet him alone," Franco says with a frown.

I smile at him. "I won't really be alone. You'll be able to see me." I hold up my wrist, showing him the tracking bracelet. "You'll be able to see me the whole time."

Franco smiles for the first time. "Perfect."

"Did you bring the drone with us?" I ask him.

He nods, gesturing toward the back of the SUV.

"Let's do a little reconnaissance before I reply to him. Maybe we can see how many people are on *Il Fantasma* before I go to the meeting point."

"I could call some other men in if we need them," Franco agrees before getting out of the driver's seat and going around to the back of the car.

I continue looking through the information that Rudy sent me while Franco sets up the drone. In a way, I understand Guiseppe's rage so clearly now.

He's my half-brother. Even though I can't imagine feeling any affection for someone as evil as Guiseppe, it makes me terribly sad to know that he is my brother. We could have grown up together as a family. If only my father hadn't been such a coward. If only Sophia's father hadn't agreed to help him hide his mistake from my mother.

I frown. My memories of my mother are complicated. She was a loving, sweet mother, but she was not allowed to have much say over my childhood.

I was raised to be a weapon, to be the fulfillment of the destiny that my father wanted to secure for his legacy. Now that I knew that Guiseppe was actually my brother, I think maybe he drove me so hard, treated me so harshly, to try and ensure that Guiseppe couldn't best me and take over the family.

I sigh. I can imagine many other ways I could be spending my life. I would actually have been quite happy to have Guiseppe ruling the roost. Being a second son to a powerful man would have been a much more pleasant life than being the first, and only heir to such a powerful name.

Franco is a second son and his life has been significantly less difficult than my own in many ways. His father allowed him to choose his own path and didn't stand in his way when he chose to be my right-hand man. I would likely have had the same kind of life.

But I would not have been betrothed to Sophia, I remind myself. It occurs to me that Guiseppe likely would have been betrothed to her instead and the thought makes me feel ill. Even if my brother hadn't turned into a monster as he aged, he still had a reputation for doing terrible things to women. Sophia's father had to pay off many of the families of women he had abused, just to keep them quiet.

My stomach turns over as I realize that even if he isn't interested in sleeping with Sophia, he likely doesn't care how much he hurts her. She's just a bargaining chip to him, a pawn. He doesn't care if she lives or dies, so long as she serves her purpose.

"Ready to fly," Franco says, breaking into my dark thoughts.

I shake my head and focus on the task at hand. I can't let the past and my new understanding of it, cloud my judgment at the moment. Sophia and our child need me to be completely focused or they might die.

"Let's see what we've got going on over there." I turn my eyes toward the harbor and watch as the drone lifts into the air to spy for us. I smile grimly in appreciation for technology. In my father's day, my men would have had to sneak onto the ship and hope for the best. Now, we could at least have some more information about who was on the ship and where it was located before we attempted to send them in.

"Can you kill him?" Franco asks me as he looks at the screen that shows him what the drone sees.

"What?" I ask, confused.

"Guiseppe," Franco says as he adjusts the direction of the drone. "Can you kill him, even knowing he's your brother?"

I frown. "I don't have a choice," I say firmly.

"That's not what I said," he replies. He glances over at me for a moment, then goes back to flying the drone and taking video. "Found *Il Fantasma*," he says with satisfaction.

I ponder his words. Before I knew who Guiseppe truly was, I would have said yes without hesitation. Now, however, knowing that he was my older brother made it a lot harder to imagine doing what needed to be done.

How long had he known that we were siblings? Could we have learned to get along if that information was out in the open? Would I have treated him any differently if I had known who he truly was?

I realize that I probably would have, and the thought was concerning, given the current situation. I harden my heart, however, as I realize that he will be unlikely to feel any hesitation about killing me if the chance offers itself. In fact, that's probably his main goal in setting up this meeting. He is probably planning to kill me as soon as he has signed documents that indicate that he will be taking over the holdings that belonged to Sophia's father.

I smile in a grim way as I realize that he has probably been keeping Sophia alive just so she can sign over her portion of her father's businesses and assets.

"I'll take that as a no," Franco says in a flat tone of voice, distracted by his work with the drone. "I'll take that into consideration."

My mouth presses into a hard line. He's not wrong. I might not be capable of pulling the trigger when it comes down to it. Maybe it's just as well that I'm going to serve as a pawn in this game of Guiseppe's. My men are more than capable of taking Guiseppe out as long as we get them established on the ship before Guiseppe brings me back to face the music.

"Do what you have to. All of you," I tell Franco. "This has to end today."

Chapter Twenty-Two

Sophia

"Don't you have any sacks that don't stink of cologne?" I mutter as I stumble after Guiseppe blindly. I'm choking to death on aftershave or cologne smell again as I try to keep up with Guiseppe and his men.

"Be glad it's not cat shit or something less pleasant," Guiseppe says nastily as he gives my arm another hard yank. We have left my little cell, but I'm not sure where we are headed. We have gone down into the bowels of the ship, that much is clear, but I have no further impression of our location.

"In my day, we actually made sure that the blindfolds that we used had been soaked in urine before we used them. There's something that the human body doesn't like about the smell of urine. It's especially upsetting after a few hours of being forced to bathe in it. Many men broke without any torture, just to avoid the pee-soaked bag being put back over their head."

I roll my eyes, knowing that he can't see the rude facial expression due to the cologne-filled hood on my head. It feels kind of nice to have some privacy, to know that my eyes and my face won't give me away as I try to figure out what to do next.

I'm not sure what Guiseppe is up to, but he seems agitated and excited. I presume Angelo is coming to meet him. It's clear that they will meet here, on the ship that Guiseppe owns.

I think we must be at least two or three levels below the room where I have been struggling to stay conscious, gagging and dizzy for what feels like days. I wonder how long he will keep me in the dark. Maybe he soaked the hood in cologne just because he knew that it would make me sick.

I stumble to a stop and dry heave, my stomach trying to grapple with the smell of the hood and the fetid, sewage-like stink of the port area.

"This is truly a disgusting process," Guiseppe says with irritation, hesitating only until I have stopped making choking sounds, before hustling me along again. "I can't imagine why everyone is so romantic over it."

"Creating life is beautiful," I say fervently. "It's a privilege, a journey. I don't expect you to understand."

He chuckles. "You know the biggest irony of all?" he says, grabbing my shoulders and pushing my head down. "Step in and duck at the same time," he orders me.

I do as he says, carefully, reaching out my hands just in case there is something in the way of my forward progression. My broken finger protests sharply and I bite back a cry of pain.

"I find it to be particularly hilarious that my father wanted to keep me a secret so badly that he didn't wait around to find out what I liked," he says, almost as if he's talking to himself.

"You see, I like men, so I would never have had an heir without my little brother anyhow. I would have enjoyed my time as ruler of our family and then I would have passed out of the history of our venerated family. But, he didn't even wait long enough to see if I liked women or men before he cut me out of his life."

Strangely, I feel for Guiseppe for a moment. There's real pain in his voice.

"When did you find out who your father was?" I ask as he shoves me into a chair. I feel him tying me up and I allow it. I need to keep him busy talking. I've learned that when he's talking, he's less likely to hurt me. I'm realizing that he's been lonely for so long, that having my company is making his tongue loose. I hope he might tell me something useful that will help me to get out of here.

He secures a knot more tightly, then stands up and brushes off his hands. I can hear the soft scraping of his callouses over one another.

"When father died, I was given a small box with the things that he had left to me. I was confused at the time. I didn't know the don of the Castiglia family well. Why would he leave me anything in his will?"

He snorts. "I thought it might be money or something, a thank you for all the times I had helped out the Castiglia family on raids and jobs. But that wasn't what it was at all. He wrote me a letter," Guiseppe says, his voice laden with pain. "He explained everything and said that he knew that I would understand why Angelo *had* to be the heir."

I can positively feel the rage pouring off of him. I swallow hard. I cannot show him that I am scared of him.

"A letter," he says caustically. "As if that would explain why he chose to abandon me and ignore me. As if a letter would make up for all the years that I was alone and unloved."

He yanks the hood off of my head, and I take a deep breath, then regret it. The air doesn't smell very good down here. I glance around. This part of the ship is not in great repair and I quail a little at what look like bloodstains on the walls and the metal floor.

"What did the letter say?" I ask, swallowing hard. I am actually curious. Being forced to spend so much time with Guiseppe has made me wonder more and more about what turned him into this kind of monster. That, and it's hard to hang onto consciousness with all of my injuries, the thirst and the exhaustion. Talking to him helps keep me going.

Guiseppe sneers. "He apologized for taking away my birthright from me. He tried to explain that I wasn't of pure blood. It's like that fantasy book with the kids who are wizards...what did they call the kids who weren't real wizards?"

"Mudbloods," I supplied helpfully.

He glances at me and grins. "Yes...that. Anyhow, he also told me that he knew that your father had treated me so well that I didn't feel any lack. After all, I was a right-hand man. What else could I want?"

I set my mouth in a thin line. Clearly, that had not been enough, and I supposed that I really couldn't blame him.

Guiseppe's phone chimes in his pocket and he smiles. "Your lover is on his way to the meeting location. I can't wait to bring you two together again. Like a matchmaker, no?"

I look him in the eye, wondering how his brain works. What is he thinking? Does he think that Angelo will give in to his demands? I don't believe for a second that my husband will let him have what he wants. He always has some kind of plan in the works. I would happily let Guiseppe have anything he wanted, just to get out of here, but Angelo is not likely to feel the same way.

"Sit tight," Guiseppe says with a slightly unhinged laugh, and then he leaves, presumably to meet Angelo.

I close my eyes as my vision swims. I'm barely hanging on by a thread at this point. I think my wounds are becoming infected due to lack of attention and I'm increasingly scared for my child. I don't honestly believe that any of us are going to get out of this alive. I'm losing hope and I'm so numb that I almost don't care.

I start to give in to the desire to just sleep, just go to sleep, and never wake up. But then, I hear a noise. Fearing rats or perhaps the presence of one of Guiseppe's men, I open my good eye a crack, looking toward the door.

It's jiggling as someone pulls the deadbolt, and I suck in a deep breath, my heart racing. Guiseppe would not have come back so soon. Something else is going on.

As I feign unconsciousness, the door opens slowly. My heart feels like it's in my throat, suffocating me. The door swings open a little and I nearly cry with relief when I see Franco poke his head inside.

"Shh," he says quietly to me, moving quickly toward me and starting to untie me. "We have all the men under control, but we need to wait for him to bring Angelo here so we can spring the trap."

"Trap?" I say hazily. He's making concerned noises as he looks at all of my wounds. He hands me a bottle of water. I have no idea where he got it from, but I grab it and greedily drink from it.

"Slowly, slowly," he cautions me. "Or you'll be sick."

"I've been gagging and retching for days," I say in between sips of water.

"Is the baby...?" he asks me, his voice trailing off.

I press a hand to my waist. "Fine, I think. But not because of Guiseppe's thoughtfulness. "He's a madman, Franco."

He nods. "I know. He's Angelo's brother."

I nod. "He told me. It's terrible. What a mess."

"A mess that will be taken care of soon," Franco promises. He pulls out some pain medication and passes it to me. "Over the counter. Safe for the baby. I checked."

I take it and swallow it around the lump in my throat. Being hydrated is working wonders for my overall physical well-being and now my fear is back full force.

"I'm able to walk," I say, rising from the chair. "Let's go get ready to attack Guiseppe."

Franco shakes his head. "There's no better place to trap him than here. Just sit tight. We'll take him out when he brings Angelo down to you. You can just act like you're tied up when he first walks in so that he doesn't realize we've come around behind him."

"But…" I start to argue. Franco glances at his phone and curses in Italian.

"They're on the move," he says. "Get back in the chair and just pretend to be tied up. We will take him out as soon as he steps into the room, don't worry."

I open my mouth to protest, but Franco is gone, locking the door behind him. I will have some words with that man when I'm out of here. This cannot possibly be the best way to handle this, but what choice do I have now?

I sit still, the thunder of my heart filling my ears and drowning out all other noise around me. Finally, after what feels like forever, I think that I hear voices.

I strain my ears and I'm finally able to recognize Angelo's deep voice speaking in reply to something that Guiseppe has said. My heart soars. He sounds like he's all right. Maybe this will work after all.

"I just need you both to sign the documents handing the business holdings over to me," Guiseppe is saying.

"Seems only fair," Angelo says readily, his tone smooth, unbothered. "After all, you were supposed to be the don of our family. I'm sorry about what our father did to you."

I think that I hear real sincerity in Angelo's voice. He probably is experiencing the same mismatched emotions about Guiseppe's story. The man is deranged but he was treated very poorly by both of our fathers.

"It's nice to finally be able to speak about who I am in the open," Guiseppe says. His voice sounds very close now and the door rattles in the frame.

I slump down in the chair, acting like I am barely conscious. The element of surprise is all we have going for us here and I believe Franco, that there is a plan in place. I can't make a mess of the plan by seeming too alert.

I peer out from under my lashes as the door slowly swings open. Guiseppe gestures for Angelo to step in first. I see him hesitate. This was clearly not part of the plan. They look at one another for a few beats and a slow smile spreads across Guiseppe's countenance. I know that smile. It's the smile that he wears right before he inflicts pain.

I jolt upright in the chair, ready to spring into action, and Guiseppe's gaze jerks to mine, his eyes going wide. He can tell that something is wrong.

"Angelo!" I cry, but it's too late.

Guiseppe grabs Angelo around the neck, pressing a gun to my husband's temple.

Chapter Twenty-Three

Angelo

The muzzle of the gun is cold where it rests against my temple. My mind works furiously as I look at my wife. She bolted up out of the chair she was slumped in, but halted dead when she realized that Guiseppe could kill me in an instant.

"I knew that you would have a trick or two up your sleeves," Guiseppe says nastily.

He starts to back away from the room that Sophia is standing in, dragging me back toward the deck of the ship. Sophia follows slowly, cautiously, her hands spread in front of her to show that she doesn't have a weapon. I notice that one of her eyes is swollen shut and she is covered in cuts and bruises. I feel impotent rage seeing her in this state.

"Guiseppe, it doesn't have to be like this," she says placatingly. "I don't need to keep my father's holdings. I really will sign them over to you. You can have it all. The Agostini name is a shell, a husk, without my father."

Guiseppe snarls and drags me after him up the stairs. "I don't believe either of you for a second," he announces, forcing me more quickly up the stairs. Sophia trails after us, her eyes wide, her chest heaving a little as she draws breath. She must be in so much pain.

I hear a clamor of sound and notice from the corner of my eye that Franco and a few of my men have come out of their hiding spots to stand behind Sophia.

Guiseppe wrenches his arm more tightly around my neck, making me cough as I try to breathe. "Don't you fucking make a move to help your boss," he hisses. "Big brother has things under control," he goes on.

He drags me up the last flight of narrow, metal steps and the breeze off the water hits us, tearing at our clothing.

"You see," Guiseppe says nastily, "I never really intended to just *trade* you power for power. You're all fools if you thought I would ever do that. No, I think it's time for a new era for the Cosa Nostra. An era without worries about who is of pure blood or who is good enough to lead. After all, if the hand that holds the gun is steady, who cares about the color of the blood flowing through its veins."

He laughs wildly, pleased with his own logic. We've come right up to the edge of the ship opposite where the gangway leads down to the docks.

"You've heard of the old-fashioned cement shoes trick, I presume?" Guiseppe says in my ear. "Well, when you own a ship like this one, you can just sail out of port to take care of business and 'accidentally' lose a shipping container over the side. Easy peasy. So tidy. I love the advancements in technology that are available to us now, compared to my youth."

I let him ramble and look at Sophia. She has been slowly, carefully moving around to the side of us. Franco and the other men are clustered in front of us, clearly trying to make sure that Guiseppe doesn't notice her absence.

"I'm going to kill you both, as it turns out," Guiseppe goes on pragmatically. "Maybe them too, I guess. They annoy me. There's plenty of room in the container for all of you," he tells us, dragging me back a few more steps.

I can see Sophia getting ever closer, her steps silent, her eyes intent on Guiseppe.

Suddenly, he wraps his arm around my neck so tightly that I see spots floating in front of my vision. He shoots Sophia, who cries out and crumples to the deck.

"Bitch!" he snarls, then waves the gun in the direction of Franco and the others, who had started swarming forward. "Stay there, or I will kill your boss as well. I'm not done explaining myself to all of you. It feels good to be heard, you know. No one ever fucking listens to me."

His arm relaxes slightly as he speaks and I look down at Sophia as best as I can. She's still lying flat, but I can see her fingers curling as she gathers herself, ready to move. Heartened by this, I start struggling as hard as I can, trying to get free despite the lack of oxygen that is making me clumsy and slow.

Guiseppe is strong for an older man, and tenacious. Perhaps his insanity is giving him super-human strength. I feel his arm slipping, but then the gun is pressed hard to my temple again, digging in.

"Fine!" Guiseppe shrieks in my ear. "If you don't want to listen, you can simply fuck off and get out of my way!"

I feel his fingers move as he prepares to squeeze the trigger, but then, suddenly, his arm falls away and he screams loudly, the sound making my ears ring.

I stumble away dizzily, the blood rushing back into my head as he releases me. I land hard on one knee and look back to see Sophia with her teeth clenched in Guiseppe's hand that is holding the gun, hanging on for dear life as he pummels her with his free hand.

Blood is running down her side from the wound in her shoulder and her lips are red with Guiseppe's blood as she grinds her teeth together as hard as she can. They stumble dangerously toward the railing, Guiseppe fetching up against it and nearly tumbling them over the edge.

My heart practically stops as he tries to throw Sophia over the edge, but she grabs onto his arm more tightly, refusing to let go. He drops the gun, grappling with her with both hands. I see it lying so close to me, but before I can make a move to snatch it up, Sophia lets go of Guiseppe's hand and dives for the gun. He kicks at her, a stream of florid Italian curses spilling from his lips as he cradles his hand.

She takes a blow to the side of her head, but she seemingly ignores it, falling on the gun and picking it up.

She sits on the ground, staring up at Guiseppe, who is cradling his wounded hand and glaring at her. Slowly, Sophia rises to her feet, covered in blood, clearly in pain, her long, dark hair tangling in the wind. She holds up the gun with a steady hand despite the blood coating her fingers and the injuries to her hands.

"Sit on the railing," she says to him, her voice flat, calm, in control.

"You fucking bitch!" Guiseppe roars, looking at his injured hand "My hand!"

She tilts her head to the side like a predator. "It won't matter in hell," she says matter-of-factly. "Sit on the railing, you piece of shit."

"Or what?" he demands. "Will you tell me about how *bad* I've been? Moralize to me a little bit about being a true Sicilian? Tell me how much it means to you that you, a woman, are forcing me to my knees?"

She sighs and shoots him in the foot. He screams and stumbles back against the railing again, looking down at his foot in shock. "Do it, or I will keep shooting you until I get my way," she says in that same perfectly controlled voice.

He starts to struggle to do as she has ordered, fear finally clear on his face.

"You know," she says to him thoughtfully. "In a way, I do feel bad for you. You were treated very poorly by both of our fathers. You deserved better."

He finally makes it into a seated position on the railing, his eyes trained on her as she speaks.

"The problem is, Guiseppe," she says, moving over a few steps to line up her shot. "Is that you are as mad as a rabid dog. There's nothing anyone can do to fix you. So I will just have to put you down."

She prepares to take her shot, when suddenly, I see Guiseppe's hand move.

"Sophia!" I shout at the same time as I hear the gunshot.

The knife that Guiseppe had been in the act of pulling out of his pocket clatters to the deck as his body tumbles backward and vanishes. I just have time to register his sightless eyes and the bloody hole in the center of his forehead before he disappears. There's a small delay and then a distant splash as his body falls into the water.

"Good riddance," Sophia says, then her eyes roll back, and she faints dead away.

Chapter Twenty-Four

Sophia

What is that beeping? I think with irritation.

I try to open my eyes, but they feel like they are glued shut.

"I think she's waking up."

Angelo? Is that his voice? I try to turn my head in his direction, but I can't seem to move it.

"She did well in surgery," another voice says. "However, she has suffered so many injuries she will need to stay here for a few days so we can be sure that she's stable."

"I understand."

That is definitely Angelo's voice. I swim harder toward the surface of my consciousness. I need to see him. I want to know what is going on.

When I'm finally able to crack my eyes open, the light in the room blinds me, and I wince, closing my eyes again.

"Hello, *Tesoro mio*," he says to me, leaning forward to press a kiss to my forehead.

My tongue feels too thick to speak and I suddenly remember my mouth being filled with Guiseppe's blood. I gag a little, pushing away the memories. I'm not ready to deal with them yet.

I open my eyes again and Angelo's handsome face swims into view. He's smiling gently at me as he reaches out to push my hair back from my face.

"The...baby..." I manage to say, my voice little more than a hoarse whisper.

He grins. "Fine as can be. You did a good job of keeping that baby safe, my love."

"I'm sorry...I..." I start to try to explain about the baby but start coughing. Pain flares to life everywhere in my body and I gasp and writhe.

"Shh," he says to me, reaching behind him for a cup of water with a straw in it. "It's fine. There wasn't time to tell me. Guiseppe told me, as it turns out, while he was threatening me. It doesn't make me any less happy about it."

I look up at him as I sip at my water. He has a couple of bruises on his face, but otherwise he looks no worse for wear. I take stock of all of the various aches and pains that are affecting me. I realize I heard someone talking with Angelo about a surgery and I look around the room to see if the doctor or nurse is still present.

"Good to see you back with us," a male voice says, and I look to my right and see Alessio Ricci looking down at me with a smile on his face. "I scrubbed in on the surgery to remove the bullet from your shoulder," he tells me, giving my fingers a squeeze.

I squeeze them back, and wince.

He grins. "See? I told you she'd be as good as new in no time if she can already use her fingers with no trouble. Rest up," he says. "I'll see you tomorrow." He waggles his fingers at us and leaves the room.

"Doc wanted to help with your surgery. I'm glad that the hospital agreed," Angelo says.

"Didn't they have lots of questions?" I whispered roughly, coughing again.

Angelo shakes his head. "No. We took you to a hospital that my father helped to fund. They don't ask questions about...these kinds of things."

I nod once, a small bob of my head, because doing anything else feels unreasonable due to the pain flaring through my body on and off when I'm not even moving around.

"Is she asleep?"

This is a new male voice, one that I don't recognize. I squint, trying to force my tired eyes to focus and I see a smallish, slender man walking up to my bed.

"Rudy," Angelo says fondly, grabbing his hand and shaking it before drawing him in for a back-slapping hug. I watch them for a moment, trying to place this newcomer and failing. "We wouldn't have made it out of this one without you. I can't repay you for your help…and for coming out of retirement.

The man who Angelo called Rudy just shakes his head and steps out of the hug. "It was nothing. It was the least I could do for a dear, childhood friend."

Childhood friend? I frown, trying to figure out what on earth is going on. I stare at Rudy as he walks closer to me. As I meet his gaze, my sluggish brain tells me that he is familiar, but I just can't figure out why.

"You probably don't remember me well, Sophia," Rudy says to me, "but we grew up together."

I frown, reaching back into my memories. I suddenly recall a young boy with spiky, messy brown hair. We were playing with toys and he was telling me about how he wanted to take his mom's computer apart, but she kept saying no to him.

"You're that Rudy?" I say, remembering him for the first time in years.

He smiles, the expression softening his sharp features and making him far more approachable. "In the flesh," he says, opening his arms a little. "I helped dig up the intel on Guiseppe that these guys needed to come rescue you."

"Thank you," I say. I barely remember this man, but he cared enough about me to help rescue me from Guiseppe. I keep being bowled over by signs of the care and love that my Italian family held for me, in spite of my mother taking us away and putting us into hiding. It feels good to realize that I am not alone, not even close to alone as it turns out.

"I hear that you need a right-hand man," Rudy says. "I know I'm not the usual kind of big, tough-guy type that does these things, but I think we would make a good team."

I smile at him. "We like to buck the trends around here," I whisper.

He chuckles and nods. "Well, I'll let you get some rest. We can talk about whether or not you want to have me stick around once you are out of here."

I shake my head. "You're hired. There's a lot that needs to be done. Angelo can help you get started."

He grins and nods. "Text me," he tells Angelo, and then he leaves the room.

I sigh and close my eyes. My head feels like it weighs ten tons.

"You should rest, *Tesoro mio,*" Angelo tells me fondly.

"Angelo?" I say to him drowsily, holding up my hand a little. I feel him take my fingers in his. "I love you."

He squeezes my fingers. "I love you more, *Tesoro mio.*"

"Thank you for bringing me home," I say.

"It was easy," he replies. "This is where you belong.

Epilogue

Sophia

I rub a hand over my pregnant belly. I'm just starting to really show, but I'm not that uncomfortable yet, thank God. We wouldn't have been able to have fun on this trip if I was late in my pregnancy. You have to walk *everywhere* in Europe.

We've been traveling around for two weeks, checking off bucket list items as we go. I showed Angelo all of my old haunts and my favorite places in the UK for starters and then we picked from a list of other places we had always wanted to see. We were always going to end up in France, however, to make sure that I got to check off a big item on my list.

I lean against the railing of the Juliet balcony at our hotel and just stare at the Eiffel Tower in all of her glory. It's so beautiful here. I can't believe we are going to be eating in the tower tonight.

My mother and I had planned to visit the Eiffel Tower when we first fled to France, but we would never have been able to afford to eat there at the time, not when my mother was trying to hide our location from my father so carefully.

"It's incredible," Angelo says behind me, stroking a hand down my back and then leaning around to kiss the side of my neck. He pulls me backward into the room, partially closing the shutter-style doors onto the balcony. There are other buildings all around us and my heart races as he slips a hand into my yoga pants and tickles my most intimate self.

It might be the pregnancy hormones or the fact that we have gotten closer than ever over the past month, but I am instantly wet for him.

"What if someone sees?" I ask him, looking back at him in question as he slips my pants off and then tugs off my shirt.

"Let them," he says to me, his voice a rumble in my ear. "You have to get dressed for dinner soon anyhow. I'm helping you out."

I laugh and roll my eyes. "Oh, sure," I say to him.

"Aren't I?" he asks me as he dips two fingers inside of me and starts to work his magic.

I gasp and grab onto the shutters for purchase as my legs tremble and my insides turn liquid in response to his touch.

"We don't want to be late," he murmurs to me, and then I feel him step behind me. His hardness caresses my clit, as I arch back into him like a cat enjoying being stroked.

"Can't have that," I mutter back, tilting my head back.

He presses into me in one long thrust, wrapping his hand around my throat and sucking my earlobe into his mouth. He nips at it as he starts to thrust, his other hand coming up to cup a breast and squeeze it.

"Angelo," I moan, arching my back to take him deeper. It's always like this. I can never get enough of him. Within moments of having an orgasm, I just want him again. I wonder if it will always be this way.

"Good lord, *Tesoro mio,*" he says to me, allowing me to fall forward so that he can grab my waist as he pounds into me. "Good God, you feel amazing."

My breasts sway as he fucks me and I look at the Eiffel Tower through lowered eyelids as the pleasure builds within me. I feel my orgasm hovering, but he abruptly pulls out of me and steps back.

I turn my mouth down in a frustrated frown, but then he catches my hand and twirls me around to face him. "I want to see it too," he says with a teasing smile sucking my lip into his mouth and nipping it gently.

He deposits me on the little dining table in our suite of rooms, scattering napkins and the table runner all over. He steps in between my legs and thrusts inside of me right away, making me cry out and arch away from the table.

He grabs my hips again, sliding me toward the edge of the table and moving faster. He looks down at me with lust-hazed eyes, his glasses sliding down his nose ever so slightly.

"Come for me, *Tesoro mio,*" he says to me and reaches down to touch my clit.

I come apart instantly, arching and spasming on the table, grabbing the edge of it for purchase as my body crackles with pleasure.

"Perfect. Beautiful," he says in Italian, before allowing himself to take his own release. He slumps over me on the table, catching himself with one hand as the pleasure shakes through him. His hair has grown longer as we have been traveling and it tickles my breasts, which grow more sensitive every day.

He presses a trembling kiss to the small mound of our child, growing in my belly and then looks up at me, his green eyes very bright.

"Do you think that it's a girl or a boy?" he asks me. His cock twitches a few times inside of me, and I clench it with my inner walls companionably in response.

"I think it's a boy," I say to him. "Although I keep telling the universe that I also want to have a girl someday, I think it's a boy."

"Hello, little Castiglia," he says to my stomach, before pressing another kiss to it. "Are you ready to go and eat at a Michelin-star restaurant, you spoiled creature?"

I giggle. "Good thing we are doing this now," I say as Angelo rises and pulls out of me. He helps me to slither off the table and back onto my feet. "There is no way that a toddler would allow us to enjoy eating at the Eiffel Tower in peace."

"You say that," he tells me with a grin, "but I bet that we will have the perfect child."

I roll my eyes. "If the amount of movement I am already feeling from junior here is any indication, I doubt that very much," I say with a laugh.

"Come, *Tesoro mio,*" Angelo says to me. "We need to get dressed for dinner. I don't think that they will let you in if you are dressed like Lady Godiva."

I giggle, imagining the scene. "The French are quite eccentric. You never know."

He shakes his head. "I don't want to share you with everyone else at the restaurant. You are my dessert for after dinner."

"Oh, I see," I say with a sage nod. Then, I grow more serious. "Thank you," I tell him.

He blinks at me. "For what?"

I smile. "For giving me a family. For loving me."

His smile is blissful as he looks at me. "Oh, for that? Well, *Tesoro mio,* that comes as easily as breathing for me."

"See that it stays that way," I say, stretching up to kiss his mouth.

He makes a noise of appreciation low in his throat and then sets me away from him.

"Dress. Now. For dinner," he says, pointing at the bedroom. "Or else we will miss our reservation and I will enjoy my dessert first."

Extended Epilogue

Sophia

I have suffered through a lot of pain in my life, but nothing else prepared me for this. I have never been in so much pain, or been so tired in my life. Not even when I was fighting for my life on Guiseppe's ship.

"You can do this," Angelo says to me, holding my hand as I bear down again, trying to push as hard as I can despite my exhaustion.

I glare at him. "Your overeager spawn couldn't bother to wait until I got my epidural. Don't tell me I can do this!"

He grins at me, unrepentant in the face of my frustration with him. "Are you too weak to give birth?" he taunts me, trying to will me into being angry enough to get through this labor. I know what he's doing, but my patience is so frayed that it actually works.

"Fuck you," I whisper at him. The nurse closest to me blinks in surprise, then smiles.

She pats my leg. "Atta girl," she says before withdrawing to enter some notes in the computer nearby.

"You're crowning," my OBGYN says excitedly.

I glare at her bowed head. I resent her excitement when all I feel is pain, nausea, and bone-deep exhaustion.

"Another couple of pushes and you will be done," Angelo tells me. He presses a kiss to my sweaty brow and I soften a little toward him just before the next painful contraction tears through me.

I've been practicing my Italian, and I switch away from English to roundly curse everything about existence, my body, and my husband as I bear down again. I add a little flourish about Angelo's giant head and the fact that he clearly has gifted our child with this unfortunate trait.

"That sounded so beautiful," my doctor says, looking up at me with a grin. "I'm sure it was all cuss words, but it sounded really pretty."

"Romance languages," Angelo says with a shrug. "The best way to curse the heavens and sound polite while you do it." He turns toward me again. "Break every bone in my hand, *Tesoro mio*," he goads me. "Show me that you can hurt me."

"I wish I had the strength to deck you right now," I grumble, allowing my body to tell me to push again. I give a little gasp of relief as I realize that it's over…I've done it. I fall back against the bed, gasping, listening to everyone else in the room cheering and celebrating my good work.

"Ready to hold your son?" my doctor asks with a grin before placing the slimy, slippery body of my child, wrapped in a towel, on my chest.

My arms come up automatically to catch my child and I expect to be revolted at the mess, but I'm not. I'm not at all. I instantly feel the most overwhelming rush of affection for the messy little bundle in my arms. I reach up and stroke back the damp mop of curly black hair on his head. Just as I thought, his head is huge.

"Are all of our children going to have bowling balls for heads?" I ask thoughtfully as I stroke the hair on my child's head.

My doctor laughs. "Probably," she says. "I'd love to lie to you, but that tends to be a consistent feature if even one of them has a huge head."

"It's all the brains in there," Angelo says proudly, and I snort. "What?" he says to me with an unrepentant smile. "You know you're the smart one around here. That means it's your fault that he has a big head, not my fault."

I giggle in spite of my exhaustion. Angelo and I have settled into a routine that includes lots of verbal sparring, which is often quite fun for me. I love ribbing him and he loves ribbing me back. It's gotten us through a lot of really tough times over the past six months.

It had taken quite a while to settle down the men who had worked for my father. They had been reluctant to be guided by a woman. I had spent a lot of time dragging my heavily pregnant self to meetings, arguments, and flat-out fights, just to make sure that my word was law.

We had removed a few men who were clearly never going to agree to my terms or my guiding hand. I hadn't asked much about what Rudy and Franco did with them. I didn't really care, to be honest. They were my father's men and I didn't owe them much in the way of loyalty. There were only a few key players who mattered to me and the rest could go hang if they didn't like my tenure as don.

"Are we still naming him Rudolpho?" Angelo asked me as he reached out to tentatively touch the crown of our baby's head.

I nod. "He saved the day when we needed him most. It's the least we can do." I think of Rudy and all the hard work that he has done to secure my place in my father's seat of power. He has been invaluable to our efforts and he has proven himself to be one of the best friends I could ever have.

"Knock knock!"

I look toward Justine's voice and smile as my friend comes prancing into the delivery room in tall stilettos and designer jeans. Justine never looks anything less than perfect and apparently sitting for hours in the hospital waiting area hasn't dimmed her fashion-model presentation a bit.

"Oh my God! His hair!" she gushes as she hurries over and examines him from every angle. She reaches back to clasp Franco's hand, yanking him closer. "Look at how beautiful he is! I can't wait until we have a baby!"

Franco looks a little green around the gills, and I chuckle. He and Justine got engaged recently, but I don't think he's quite ready for babies or homemaking yet.

"We will name our first girl Sarah of course," Justine rambles on, and my eyes unexpectedly fill with tears. "Oh, gosh, I'm sorry," she says quickly, pressing her hand to mine where it is cradling Rudolpho's body. "We don't have to do that if you aren't okay with it."

I shake my head, the tears spilling down my cheeks. "No, no. I love it," I say with a watery smile. I wave my free hand. "Pregnancy hormones," I say, but I know it's not that, not really. It means so much to me that Justine still remembers who I was when I was living as Sarah.

"Then it's decided," Justine says happily. She turns to Franco. "Can we start trying now? I want our babies to grow up together."

Franco is white as a sheet and he swallows hard. Angelo chuckles and pokes him in the ribs with his elbow. "Just say yes," he suggests. "It's easier in the long run."

"Sure," Franco manages to choke out.

Justine claps and dances around in a circle, her heels clacking on the hospital room floor. "I'm *so* excited!" she squeals. "Our baby is going to be so, so, so beautiful!"

I look over her head at Angelo and we share a smile. I don't think either of us ever gets tired of how *normal* our lives really are. We worked hard to secure a future for ourselves and also for those who are loyal to us. We won't treat people the way that our fathers did. We want to create a family joined by loyalty and a desire to stay safe and be cohesive.

"I love you," I mouth to my husband.

"I love you forever, *Tesoro mio,*" he mouths back.

My heart is full and a piece of it is now resting on my chest, ready to take on a brave new life.

I think of my parents and close my eyes. *Thank you*, I think to the both of them. *Thank you for helping to make sure that everything turned out all right in the end.*

The end.

Did you like this book?
Then you'll LOVE Surprise Baby for the Mafia Boss.
Scan the QR code to start reading Surprise Baby for the Mafia Boss NOW!

I'm knocked up by the man I could never have.
He's a ruthless Italian Don.
And my best friend's brother.

When your lifelong bestie is a mafia princess,
You end up intertwined with the family, like it or not.

Her big brother grew tall, chiseled, and powerful right
before my eyes.
It's been pure torture to have him so close, but so
off-limits.

But when he needs to impress a rival family, he asks me to
pretend *I'm his.*

I know the risks but I can't say no.
Even if it means I'll lose my best friend.

As we fake our marital bliss, I see it in his devilish eyes;
I've gone from invisible to *he'll never let me go.*

But now I'm growing a surprise that threatens to destroy
the trust we've built.
This pregnancy is an accident, not a trap... *I swear.*

Sneak Peek...

Sneak Peek – Chapter One

Surprise Baby for the Mafia Boss

LUCA

I watch myself in the mirror as I pull my jacket on, slowly, savoring the feeling of being wrapped in a cloud. I splurged heavily on this Vicuña wool suit, but I need the men I'm meeting to take me seriously.

My steel blue gaze stares back at me as I straighten myself up, pulling my shoulders back and taking in a deep breath. Tonight's meeting is about securing a new product source, something big for the family business.

Going home with this deal in hand will finally show the whole family that I'm more than just the pretty face of this business.

I've been trying to get my older brother to allow me to take on new meetings like this for three years, but only now does he feel I'm mature enough. Which is rich coming from him. He's been doing this since he was much younger than me.

But it's always been assumed that he could do it while I needed to be micromanaged. This is the perfect opportunity to prove him wrong.

I crack my knuckles, enjoying the sound of my bones grating against one another. I imagine wrapping my fingers around the rising violence inside of me, strangling it back.

It has always been like this for me; the struggle to contain the wildness inside of me. It's part of why my brother, Enzo, has never trusted me to take on business deals on my own.

I admit that violence is like a high to me. Giving in to the wild thing inside of me always feels like a release. It's almost orgasmic, and I often get carried away.

But that doesn't mean that I like being used by my family like a beautiful sword that they almost never release from its scabbard.

I try to tame my unruly hair one final time before I turn away from the mirror. I always keep the sides short, but my barber left a little much on top at my last visit. My attempts are futile, these dark locks have a mind of their own.

As I grab my wallet and phone, I feel vibrating in my hand and realize I'm getting a call. It's my brother. No surprise, he's probably just trying to control this deal and how I handle it.

I love my family, but their lack of trust in my abilities really boils my blood.

I hit the silence button — I'll call him back after the meeting, let him know just how well it went without his help. I head out the door, feeling confident and almost smug.

I arrive at the posh bar where our business contacts decided to meet and slip through the door like a shadow. The cute little redhead at the hostess desk gives me a simpering look when I walk up to greet her.

I tell her who I have come to meet with, and she leads me to a private room at the back of the establishment with a phenomenal view of the city through the floor-to-ceiling windows.

I watch her plump ass swaying as she walks in front of me, and I muse on the thought of yanking her into one of the other rooms along the way to have my way with her.

I shake the thought away, however. That kind of distracted thinking is exactly why my brother doesn't trust me.

Stop thinking with your cock and your fists, Luca, he has said to me more than once.

I pull my shoulders back and settle for giving the redhead a wink before I saunter into the room she has led me to. I ignore her disappointed pout.

Pretty girls are a dime a dozen. She doesn't matter to me.

The meeting does go well.

These men are no pushovers, but with a little charm, and a lot of liquor, they are reasonable. I have a good list of negotiations to take back to the family so we can set this all in motion.

After they've left I throw back a few extra celebratory drinks before heading back to my room.

As I stumble back into my room, I knock my knee on the table in the hallway and swear loudly. I kick it over and feel an immense amount of satisfaction when it crashes over with a loud noise, sending the vase of flowers on top of it down to shatter on the marble floor.

My watch says it's almost midnight, but I'm riding a wave of pride at how I just handled this meeting and I feel like I could go another twenty-four hours without sleep.

It's never easy, navigating negotiations while building trust, and keeping my wits about me. But contrary to what my brother believes, I am just as capable as he is.

If he tries to dispute my abilities after this trip, I'll laugh in his face. My sister also thinks I can't do this work, although she's usually quicker to give me the benefit of the doubt.

Thinking of my siblings reminds me to call my brother back. I can tell him his worries about my ability to handle this meeting weren't necessary.

Pulling my phone out of my pocket, I see he's tried to call me five more times. It just shows how hard he finds it to let go of the reins.

I feel a rush of resentment at this proof that he doesn't trust me at all.

He sent me here; why won't he just let me do my thing? Because he still sees me as his kid brother. That's why. I know the reason, but it still annoys the shit out of me.

It's late, but I know he'll still be awake. I find his contact in my phone and press the call button. "Fuck him," I mutter to myself with annoyance. I let myself into my hotel room and kick the door shut behind me.

My brother answers almost before the first ring. "Jesus, Luca, where the fuck have you been?" He's yelling into the phone, so I move it away from my ear and put it on speaker.

"Calm down, man, fuck. I was in the meeting I told you about and put my phone on silent. I just saw your missed calls now." I'm lying, but his anger is not something I want to be dealing with right now.

"Okay, well in the future, wherever the fuck you are, and whatever the fuck you're doing, you keep your phone on. Got it?"

I sigh. "Got it." It's an old rule — keep yourself available at all times in case of issues.

The logical part of me knows why but I don't like the pressure of knowing other people can reach me whenever they want to.

"Ok."

He sighs and his tone changes from agitation to something I can't really place. "You need to come home."

"Yeah, sure. I've only got two more meetings to do tomorrow, and then I'm wrapping it up and coming home. I'll be there by Wednesday." I gave him my itinerary before I left, so he knows this.

"No, Luca. You need to come home now." My brother is good at bossing me around, but this sounds more like a desperate plea than a command.

"What happened?" I ask, my breath quickening.

My gut tells me something's not okay, and I think about the family members at home who might have been at risk before I left for Mexico.

My brother is clearly fine, but then I think about my sister. She's usually smart and good at keeping herself out of trouble. But if anyone has tried to harm her, I'd have their heads before they knew I was even coming for them.

"I don't want to have this conversation over the phone, Luca. Can you call the pilot and arrange an early morning flight back? As soon as you're home, I'll update you."

"Nuh uh, tell me now."

"Luca, I…" My phone screen suddenly goes black, and I realize that I've forgotten to charge it.

"For fuck's sake," I growl at no one but myself and run to plug it in. It takes a full three minutes to get it back on, and I dial my brother back as soon as it allows me.

"Luca," he answers in a solemn tone, not giving me a chance to explain what just happened. "It's Nonna. She's gone."

I freeze, the weight of my brother's words sinking in like an anchor dropped to the depths of the ocean.

"Luca," he repeats. His words hang in the air, a painful echo reverberating in my mind.

Our grandmother, the anchor of our family, the woman who weathered the storms of our lives with unwavering strength, was no more.

A lump forms in my throat as I grapple with the sudden reality, one that feels inconceivable.

My mind races back to the last time I saw her, just a couple of months ago. We had laughed over coffee, discussing the places she wanted me to take her shopping upon my return. She seemed lively, full of the same vibrant energy that had defined her for as long as I could remember.

The idea that this lively, indomitable force had slipped away, leaving behind only memories, feels surreal.

"Luca?" My brother's voice interrupts the flood of memories, pulling me back to the present.

"She held on for a long time," he continues, his own voice sounding raw with grief, "but this afternoon she took her usual nap, and when her nurse went in, she was gone. It was peaceful, and she was at home where she wanted to be."

She was almost eighty-seven years old, and it was to be expected I guess. But my heart feels like it isn't even beating anymore.

I just never thought of her ever leaving us. Not really. She always seemed so full of life. It was only in the last year or so that she even seemed sick, and she never let that fully affect her.

"Okay," I manage to utter, the word escaping my lips like a fragile whisper.

The room feels smaller, suffocating, as if the air has been sucked out. After losing my parents at a time when my core memories were still forming, Nonna Ginny became my constant, the guiding force that helped me navigate the tumultuous waters of life.

She wasn't the stereotypical grandmother seen on TV, baking cookies and knitting in a rocker chair. No, Nonna Ginny was a force of nature, a woman who demanded respect and gave unwavering love in return.

My mind races through the lessons she imparted, the values she instilled. Loyalty above all, was her mantra, and she taught us how to stand by each other as family.

Nonna was the compass that guided us through the murky waters of life's challenges, showing us the importance of holding on to each other in times of need.

She also had no problem telling all of us — family, friends, business associates — exactly what she thought about our attitudes, and giving us tips to improve them if she felt that's what we needed.

The realization that I could no longer seek her advice, share a laugh, or find solace in her comforting presence suddenly hits me like a tidal wave.

"Luca?" Enzo says to me, his tone cautious. "Luca, don't freak out."

I stare at the phone in my hand like I've never seen one before. I end the call and set my phone on the bed with shaking fingers.

The chaos inside of me feels like deep, dark water sucking me under. I grip my temples, trying to calm down, trying to get a hold of myself.

Nonna wasn't just a grandmother; she was the heartbeat of our family, and I already know that her absence will leave an ache that words can't capture.

I'm not sure I'm ready to say goodbye to the most important person in my life.

She was the only one I told about what happened to me when I tried to get out, tried to make my own way and work outside of the family business.

A collage of images rages through my mind: pain, unwilling attraction, injuries I couldn't tell anyone about. Hiding my shame, unwilling to admit that I needed to escape, break the cycle.

The pain coalesces inside of me and then implodes. A ragged scream tears from my throat, and I throw the bedside table to the ground, the lamp smashing to the floor, scattering crystal pendants across the floor.

I tear the room apart, the destruction the only possible balm for my rage, my fear, my anguish. When I finally calm down enough to stop breaking things, I stand in the destruction of my hotel room, panting.

My palm feels wet, and I hold up my hand to see that it's bleeding, a fresh cut tearing through the sensitive flesh. I mindlessly pull off my designer tie and wrap it around my hand.

I grab my phone from the mess on the bed and arrange for my jet to be ready to fly at dawn.

Then I curl up in the middle of the bed, cradling my injured hand against my chest, and drop into an uneasy sleep.

Scan the QR code to continue reading Surprise Baby for the Mafia Boss...

About the Author

Demi Ryder creates sexy dark mafia worlds that will make you weak in the knees. Deliciously dangerous alphas and the fiery heroines who fall prey in their naughty games are calling you.

Don't be scared. It's morally gray and twisty here, but there's always a happy ending.

Scan the QR code to follow Demi on Amazon (click that "+Follow" button!)

Scan the QR code below to join my newsletter and get a SPICY gift.

Printed in Great Britain
by Amazon